OTHER YEARLING BOOKS YOU WILL ENJOY:

THE MOFFATS, *Eleanor Estes*
RUFUS M., *Eleanor Estes*
THE MOFFAT MUSEUM, *Eleanor Estes*
ALL-OF-A-KIND FAMILY, *Sydney Taylor*
ALL-OF-A-KIND FAMILY DOWNTOWN, *Sydney Taylor*
ALL-OF-A-KIND FAMILY UPTOWN, *Sydney Taylor*
MORE ALL-OF-A-KIND FAMILY, *Sydney Taylor*
ELLA OF ALL-OF-A-KIND FAMILY, *Sydney Taylor*
THE HAPPY LITTLE FAMILY, *Rebecca Caudill*
SCHOOLHOUSE IN THE WOODS, *Rebecca Caudill*

YEARLING BOOKS/YOUNG YEARLINGS/YEARLING CLASSICS are designed especially to entertain and enlighten young people. Patricia Reilly Giff, consultant to this series, received the bachelor's degree from Marymount College. She holds the master's degree in history from St. John's University, and a Professional Diploma in Reading from Hofstra University. She was a teacher and reading consultant for many years, and is the author of numerous books for young readers.

For a complete listing of all Yearling titles, write to Dell Readers Service, P.O. Box 1045, South Holland, IL 60473.

THE
MIDDLE MOFFAT

Eleanor Estes

Illustrated by Louis Slobodkin

A Yearling Book

Published by
Dell Publishing
a division of
Bantam Doubleday Dell Publishing Group, Inc.
666 Fifth Avenue
New York, New York 10103

ISBN: 0-440-70028-0

Reprinted by arrangement with Harcourt Brace Jovanovich, Publishers

Printed in the United States of America

June 1989

10 9 8 7 6 5 4 3 2 1

KRI

To Clarence

CONTENTS

1

JANE, THE MIDDLE MOFFAT

"This is Jane, the middle Moffat," said Jane, trying to act as though she were Mama, introducing her to one of the ladies she sewed for. That is not the way Mama actually introduced her to these ladies. Mama merely said, "This is Jane." She never added, "the middle Moffat." Jane was adding that now to see how it sounded.

She was sitting under the big elm tree at the

end of the long green lawn in front of the Moffats' new house. In her lap was a round rag rug she was crocheting. It kept humping up in the middle. Right now it looked more like a giant's skull cap than a rug. Perhaps when all the Moffats began to walk on it the hump would flatten out. They would stand on it often enough because it was going to be placed on the burnt spot in front of the pot-bellied stove.

"I'm the middle Moffat," Jane repeated. "Not the oldest, not the oldest son, not the youngest, just the middle."

Sylvie was the oldest Moffat. When Mama introduced Sylvie to the ladies who came to try on, she always said, "This is Sylvie, my oldest child."

Sylvia was sweet sixteen. On her last birthday her aunt had sent her sixteen lumps of sugar

tied with pink ribbons all in a cluster. They were not to eat even though sugar was scarce.

"When you're sweet sixteen you get these things and you keep 'em," Jane explained to Rufus who looked wide-eyed at the idea of sugar you kept and did not eat.

Naturally Rufus did not know about these things. He was the youngest, just six in fact. He was in Room Two. In school he remembered to do almost everything the right way except to carry the one in arithmetic. He often forgot to do that. In the Moffats' house you were apt to hear someone say, "Watch out for Rufus because he is the littlest." Or, "Let Rufus do it first because he is the youngest." When Mama introduced Rufus to the ladies who came to try on, she said, "This is Rufus, the baby in the family."

And when Mama introduced Joey to people she would say, "This is Joey, my oldest son." Ever since Papa had died Joey had become more and more important in this family. He was thirteen. He locked the doors and closed the shutters at night. He kept the coal scuttles filled and he took care of the stoves. Joey, the oldest son.

But, when Mama introduced Jane, she just said, "This is Jane." Because Mama had not figured out that Jane was the middle Moffat. Nobody had figured that out but Jane.

"Yes. This is Jane, the middle Moffat," Jane repeated out loud, addressing nobody in particular though Catherine-the-cat gave her an inquiring glance and paused with her front paw on a grasshopper.

Why even Catherine was called Catherine-the-cat. Never just Catherine. And the sewing figure which the Moffats called Madame was usually referred to as Madame-the-bust. Jane should be called Jane, the middle Moffat. It sounded good.

Jane wound a strip of bright red cloth around her crochet hook. The middle of other things was good too, she thought. The middle of a sandwich and the middle of a pie. The middle of the night, when exciting things happened in books. The middle of the day, lunch time. The Middle Ages, though what they were Jane was not certain.

Ouch! Jane's back was getting stiff. She stretched and then settled herself comfortably against the elm tree again. If someone came walking along Ashbellows Place and asked her who she was, she was going to say, "I'm Jane, the middle Moffat." If it sounded as good to others as it did to her, she would ask Mama to introduce her that way to the ladies who came to try on.

The Moffats had not been living on this street very long, and everybody didn't know them yet. Very likely there were lots of people who would like to know who this girl was, sitting under this tree, how old she was, and what room she was in in school. Natural to want to know. She remembered when a family moved to New Dollar Street where the Moffats used to live, she would want to know the same things when she saw a strange girl.

Jane looked down the street, hoping someone would come along. Ah! Here came a girl around the corner from Pleasant Street, pulling a little boy in a red tin express wagon. The girl kept her eye on Jane all the way up the street. She walked

very slowly. Jane could see that the girl was wondering who she was. Jane raised her head and gave her an expectant and encouraging look, but waited for the girl to speak first.

She didn't though. She drew up beside Jane. She and the little boy were licking pink lollipops. They watched Jane but said nothing.

Well, thought Jane, if she doesn't ask me, I'll have to ask her.

"What's your name?" she said.

"Clara Pringle. This is my brother. Brud, we call him."

"Oh ..." said Jane. Now you ask me, she thought.

And after watching Jane for a while in silence, Clara did ask her.

"What's your name?" she finally asked. Jane was relieved. Now she could say it.

"I'm Jane, the middle Moffat," she said.

Clara's only response to this was a prolonged stare. Then she started to back up the street. She pulled Brud along the sidewalk backwards so she could watch Jane. She watched Jane all the way up the street, even forgetting her lollipop. So did Brud. In fact they watched so hard Brud nearly fell out of his wagon when Clara stumbled over a root that jutted up under the sidewalk. When they reached the corner they  stopped and watched Jane some more. Then slowly they disappeared from sight around Pleasant Street. As they disappeared from sight, Jane suddenly shouted after them:

"Jane, the middle Moffat!"

This caused the two Pringles to return to the corner (they really had not gone very far) and to sit in their express wagon where they watched Jane for a long, long time.

Jane wondered what was the matter. Didn't they like the sound of middle Moffat? However, you couldn't tell with just one person. She would try it on somebody else.

Where were all the other neighbors? My, this was a quiet street. It was a little short street, and it didn't have any other children on it at all.

Just the Moffats. Some children might move into the big house which had just been built next door. And of course there were two girls named Nancy and Beatrice Stokes who lived in the big house in back of the Moffats. But right now they were still away on their vacation. Jane wished they'd come back.

But at last here came somebody else. It was the letterman! He hadn't brought the Moffats one single letter since they lived here. Perhaps he didn't know there was a house here. The Moffats' house was set so far back from the street, he might never have noticed it. Their front porch began where other people's back porch ended. The letterman might have the idea that their lawn was just a nice little park or even an empty lot!

Besides telling the letterman that she was the middle Moffat, she would call his attention to this house of theirs. When he was right in front of this long green lawn she would stop him and make sure that he saw the little white house, a toy house, at the end of it. A surprise house! That's what the Moffats lived in now.

The nearer the letterman came, the nearer the Pringles inched their way back towards Jane. They wished to watch her from a little closer range.

Now the letterman was here.

"Hello," said Jane. "Any letters for the Moffats? We live here now. We don't live on New Dollar Street any more." But before she had a chance to add, "I'm Jane, the middle Moffat," he had shaken his head and said, "No. Not today," and tramped rapidly on, his leathery, weather-beaten face absorbed in finding the right letter in his pack for the next house.

And as the letterman disappeared in one direction, Clara Pringle slowly shoved Brud along in the other. She was sitting in the back of the wagon herself now pushing with her foot and making Bruddie steer. And now they really vanished from sight around the corner. Jane was all alone again.

An ant crawled over her bare leg and disappeared in a business-like fashion down an ant hole. Going to the middle of the earth, that's where, thought Jane. The middle of the earth was a mysterious place like the middle of the night, and the middle of the ocean too, where there very likely were water-spouts, whirlpools, and mermaids.

"I'm Jane, the mysterious middle Moffat," she tried.

No. What was there mysterious about her?

Nothing. She certainly didn't wear a mask or go around on tiptoe saying Sh-sh-sh! like Hawkshaw, the detective. Everybody knew who she was or could very easily find out. But you'd almost think there was something mysterious about her from the way that Clara Pringle was acting. There she was, back at the corner again with Brud, watching Jane. Their lollipops were gone now. Jane was tempted to shout "mysterious middle Moffat" at Clara. But she refrained. She didn't run around pretending she was a princess in disguise. Middle? Yes. Mysterious? No.

But now, here came another person. Jane recognized him. Everybody knew him. It was Mr. Buckle, the oldest inhabitant! He was ninety-nine years old and soon he would be one hundred. A century! Jane was ten. He was almost ten times ten. Phew! He was a veteran of the Civil War. He always rode on the float in the Decoration Day parade and he sat on the stage at the Town Hall for the graduation exercises. He lived on the corner of Pleasant Street. Now he came up Ashbellows Place with his short shuffling steps and his knees bent forward a little.

His face was always beaming and from a long way off you could see his bright blue eyes and the white hair falling below his cap.

As Mr. Buckle slowly moved up the street, he paused now and then to blow cotton to the birds. He always carried around cotton for the birds who liked to line their nests with it. He would take a small puff of cotton between thumb and forefinger and blow it delicately up into the air, turning this way and that so all the cotton would not be wafted in the same direction. He liked it when a sparrow caught a puff in the air before it floated to the ground.

Jane smoothed her dress and brushed away a strand of hair from her forehead. She was polite. She did not stare at the oldest inhabitant, but when she saw from beneath her lashes that he was near at hand, she looked up at him with a friendly and expectant smile. She was hoping he would ask her who she was. And that she wouldn't have to ask first the way she had Clara Pringle.

The oldest inhabitant stopped beside her and, leaning on his cane, he said very slowly and distinctly:

"Are you one of the Moffats?"

"Yes, Mr. Buckle," said Jane, feeling very shy before such an important man but wishing she had the courage to say she was the middle Moffat. If it sounded all right to the oldest inhabitant then it was a good thing to say, for he was Cranbury's most honored citizen.

Fortunately the oldest inhabitant continued. "Which Moffat are you?"

"I'm Jane . . . the mysterious middle Moffat," Jane explained. But goodness, she had said exactly what she had meant not to say. Mysterious! It just came out, that word mysterious. Now! How was the oldest inhabitant going to take this?

"I see . . ." he said, lowering his voice to a whisper. "The mysterious middle Moffat! Well," and his head began nodding slowly up and down, "what's so mysterious about you?"

"Well, I'm not really mysterious," said Jane, feeling embarrassed. "I'm just middle."

"Yes . . . ?" said Mr. Buckle as though he really needed more explanation.

So Jane went on. "Middle Moffat, that's me, is not mysterious. The middle of the night is."

"The mysterious middle Moffat is not mysterious," said the oldest inhabitant thoughtfully.

"No," agreed Jane, laughing politely.

Mr. Buckle put his finger on the side of his nose the way Hawkshaw, the detective, did in

the pictures and he beamed down at her. "But the middle of the night is ..." he went on.

"And the middle of the ocean," added Jane.

"But not the middle Moffat," he said. "Sh-sh-sh, this is all very mystifying."

"I didn't mean to say mysterious," said Jane. "See? It just came out."

"That's what makes the whole thing so very mysterious," said the oldest inhabitant.

Then Mr. Buckle pulled his cap down a little over his eyes. Again he put his finger on the side of his nose, and as he shuffled off, he said "Sh-sh-sh."

Jane bent over her rag rug. Now for goodness' sakes, what was the oldest inhabitant going to think of her? The Moffats had only just moved to this street and they were anxious to make a good impression.

Jane saw Mr. Buckle turn into his yard. Before going into the house he turned and played Hawkshaw once more. Jane decided to treat the whole matter as a game herself. She scrunched up her lips and said "Sh-sh-sh," also. Then she picked up her crocheting and went into the house, leaving Clara and Brud Pringle still staring from the corner.

"Well," Jane decided, "if it hadn't been for that one word, 'mysterious,' it would have sounded all right to say Jane, the middle Moffat."

She went into the dining room where Mama was sewing on some light green crêpe de Chine. It was a pretty color and Jane hoped there would be a little piece left over for her to make a dress for her doll.

Jane thumbed through the little black notebook where Mama kept the measurements of all the ladies she sewed for. At the beginning of the book were the ladies she had sewn for in New York before she came to live in Cranbury. Mama had all the measurements, hip, waist, length of sleeve, and length of skirt for a great many elegant ladies who used to live in the Brevoort and the Berkeley.

Now she sewed for some of the ladies in Cranbury and the last names in the book were those of the Gillespie twins. You would think because they were twins they would measure exactly the same. Not at all. There was a half inch off here, and an inch on there.

"Mama," said Jane, "is anyone coming to try on?"

"Yes, Janey," said Mama. "The Gillespie twins."

Good! The Gillespie twins! They didn't know who Jane was, and of course Mama would have to tell them. At this moment the bell rang, and Mama went to open the door. Jane followed her, saying quickly, "Mama, when you say 'This is Jane,' don't end there. Say, 'This is Jane, the middle Moffat.'"

But she didn't know whether Mama heard her or not. Mama greeted the twins and everybody went into the dining room.

"Oh, how lovely," said one of the twins. "Mrs. Moffat, you are a wonder to have thought of dressing us in pale green. With our red hair, imagine that Mrs. Weaver dressing us in pink!"

"Your hair is lovely. You should always wear green and lavender," said Mama decidedly. She knew because she had sewn for all the elegant ladies in the little black notebook.

Jane felt proud of Mama. She picked up her thimble which had rolled under the table. When she came up, Mama put her arm around her shoulders and said to the twins:

"This is Jane, the middle Moffat."

"Oh," they said. "Hello, Jane."

Jane smiled and then she went out of the house through the kitchen to the back yard. It sounded good the way Mama had said it. And she hadn't made any mistake either, like adding the word mysterious. If only the oldest inhabitant would remember the middle part and forget the mysterious part.

But he didn't.

Every time Jane met Mr. Buckle on the street he would pull his cap down over his eyes and play the game of Hawkshaw. And Jane would stoop her head and shoulders and tiptoe past him in the most mysterious way she knew. This game they played every time they saw each other, no matter where they were. There were times when Jane wished she didn't have to play this game, but she didn't know how to stop.

One day Jane decided to tell him again there was nothing mysterious about her. ". . . you see?" she said. "I don't pretend to be a princess in disguise. Just the middle Moffat. That's enough."

"Sh-sh," was all he said, going off to blow cotton to the birds.

Another warm evening all the Moffats went together to the Green to see the fireworks. Mama put on her hat with the forget-me-nots that matched her eyes, and she put on her gloves. For she had been born and brought up in New York City and she never went out without her hat and her gloves. When the Moffats arrived at the Green a big crowd had gathered and the people were eating popcorn and crackerjacks, and drinking soda water. The peanut-man's whistle rang in their ears.

On a bench beside the drinking trough sat old Mr. Buckle, enjoying the scene. Jane was walking between Mama and Sylvie. She really hoped

that this time the oldest inhabitant wouldn't see her. What would the other Moffats think of this mysterious act of hers? But Mr. Buckle did see her and he played Hawkshaw as usual. Jane smiled at him but she did not join in the game. It was the first time she hadn't since they had begun.

When they passed his bench, Mama said, "He is a wonderful old man, Mr. Buckle is. Imagine! Ninety-nine years old. Nearly a century!"

Jane felt sorry she had acted the way she had. What did it matter what the other Moffats thought? This was the oldest inhabitant and he was going to live to be one hundred. If he wanted to play detective, the least she could do was to play detective too. She ran back, said "Sh-sh-sh," tiptoed around his bench and then rejoined her family.

"Why did you do that?" they demanded.

But fortunately Jane didn't have to explain because the Roman candles and the skyrockets began. When the fireworks were over the rest of the Moffats had forgotten about Janey's odd behavior, and they all drank orange whistle before going home.

They had forgotten, but Jane hadn't. And she

wondered how she was ever going to persuade the oldest inhabitant she was not the mysterious middle Moffat but just the middle Moffat.

2

THE ORGAN RECITAL

A lot of people in the town gave the Moffats things they did not want any more. Some of these presents, such as croquet sets with half the balls missing, were a disappointment. Even these were useful though, for by combining several old sets the children almost had a complete outfit.

But some presents they liked very much. One

of their favorite presents was a collection of flat, glass-covered boxes filled with butterflies, moths, flies, dragon-flies and other insects mounted on pins. Each box was labeled with a strange name. One box was called *Musca domestica*. Just plain flies, they looked like, and why should anyone collect them, Jane wondered, and stick them on pins?

"Aren't these what we swat all the time in the kitchen?" she asked Joey.

"Look the same to me," said Joe. But he added thoughtfully, "I suppose it's all in the interest of science."

"Collecting flies is science?" Jane asked in dismay.

The Moffats were happy because they knew

they would get one hundred per cent in nature study when they took these exhibits to school. Nobody had ever had such a collection of *Insecta* as this.

Then the week that Professor Fairweather lectured to his Browning Society on Thoreau, the Moffats received quite a windfall.

Everybody in the club must read "Walden" by Thoreau, advised the professor. So the ladies went home and read "Walden." They found that Thoreau was against accumulating too many possessions. Then they started giving things away.

One of the ladies was Miss Nellie Buckle, the daughter of the oldest inhabitant. After reading Thoreau she had cleaned out her attic and what had she found? A whole lot of mildewed old books stored away. She certainly should dispose of these. First she thought of the library. But the library did not want them because they were so out of date. Then she thought of the Moffats. At first Mama refused too, for she wondered where she could put them. But the children seemed so disappointed Mama finally said, "Well, all right."

So, with Joey behind her, Miss Buckle bustled busily with her short springy steps back and forth from her house to the Moffats' house with piles of books. Now she was living the way Thoreau advocated, she told herself. She

kept shaking her head and straightening her shoulders as though she had just rid herself of a tremendous burden.

Joey piled the books on the little square porch. My, they were musty! The pages were brown with age and crackling at the edges. Even Mama was interested. She sat down on the top step and looked through the books. They were chiefly about the work of missionaries among the cannibals. Rufus and Joey loved them. And before anyone could stop him, Rufus painted the faces of all the cannibals with bright red moustaches. After Rufus had touched up the pictures with crayon, Janey never again found them as scary as she first had.

So that had been another present the Moffats liked.

But the most important present was the one Mrs. Price gave them. After Professor Fairweather's lecture on Thoreau, she too had gone home and looked about. Should she part with this? Should she part with that? Her eyes scanned the parlor. They rested lovingly on the little mahogany parlor organ. Well, that was one thing, Thoreau or no Thoreau, that she would keep. Not that she played it. But where else could she keep the photographs of all her nephews?

Since she could reach no decision as to what to give away she closed her eyes, turned herself around three times and pointed. Then she opened her eyes. No! She couldn't believe it. But yes, it was true. She was pointing right straight at that little parlor organ. She'd try again. This time she went out of the room, came back, closed her eyes, turned herself around three times and pointed. Ridiculous! Out of all the things there were in the room, here she was pointing at the organ again. A third time Mrs. Price tried this. She covered her eyes with her right arm, turned dizzily around, and pointed. She peeked out from under her arm. Incredible! Three times she had pointed at this organ. Well, all right then. If it was the organ, let it be the organ.

Mrs. Price put on her black clothes. She went next door to the Moffats' house and she asked them if they would like to have her little parlor organ.

Would the Moffats like to have Mrs. Price's little parlor organ? Well! What a question! Music! Bach! An organ! The Sunday afternoon organ recitals at Woolsey Hall! The great cathedrals and the churches! "Seated one day at the organ." These were the thoughts that raced through their heads. Other people in the town owned pianos, but they were going to own an organ. Sylvie sighed for she wished it was a piano. Still

an organ would be nice. She did not want to appear ungrateful and tried to act as pleased as the rest.

Joey, Jane, and Rufus were really very pleased. They knew they could sit right down and play something.

"I tried it on the parish house piano once," said Jane.

Now the children were all sitting on the long green lawn waiting for Mr. I. Bimber's moving man to bring the organ. The little green and white parlor was all ready for it. Joey had moved the big armchair out of the corner and Janey had dusted carefully not only that corner but the entire room. Then they had washed the windows and the room sparkled with clean curtains fluttering in the breeze.

"Do you think the organ will have one of those winding pianner stools to it?" asked Rufus. Oh, he did hope it would, so he could twirl it around and around.

"Oh, sure, it will have one of those," Joe answered confidently.

Jane was thinking they could give organ recitals. They might charge admission and the Moffats would get rich. Goodness! What was she thinking? Charge admission for music? Music should

be free like at Woolsey Hall. "Seated one day at the organ," she sang.

The moving man drove up.

"Mama, here it comes!" shouted Rufus, while Joe and Jane tried to act more dignified to impress the neighbors. Sylvie waited until the little organ was carried over and carefully backed into its corner in the green and white parlor. Then she ran out the door and down the street, saying she was going to be late to choir rehearsal. She really ran off because she did not want anyone to see the tears in her eyes. All her life she had wanted a piano and to take piano lessons and now here was this funny little organ that smelled faintly of camphor.

Mama looked out of the window after Sylvie for a moment. Then with a little sigh she went back to the dining room table where she was cutting out flannel nightgowns for Miss Buckle.

This left Rufus, Jane, and Joe to admire the organ and really give it a welcome.

"Hey," said Rufus suddenly, "it hasn't got any pianner stool."

So it didn't. Joe ran after Mr. I. Bimber's moving man. Perhaps he had forgotten to bring it. But no, that's all there was.

"Mama," wailed Rufus, "there isn't any pianner stool to this organ."

"Oh, no," Mama replied. "I forgot to tell you Mrs. Price decided in the end to keep the piano stool. She likes to sit on it when she makes her raspberry jam. She said something about not having pointed at it anyway, that she'd only pointed at the organ. I don't know what she was talking about."

"Oh, dear," said Jane ruefully. "Well, a chair will have to do." But pleasure in the organ was almost ruined for Rufus who had looked forward so to twirling a piano stool.

They set one of the straight chairs from the kitchen in front of the organ and Joey, being the oldest of the three, sat down to play.

You had to pump the pedals of this organ with your feet all the time you were playing the keys with your fingers. First Joey played the scale.

"Play something real," said Rufus.

Then by ear, Joe played with one finger "My Country, 'Tis of Thee." After that he played "Old Black Joe." Next Jane played "Old Black Joe" by ear. And finally Rufus, who had waited very impatiently for his turn, slowly picked out the notes for "My Country, 'Tis of Thee" with his chubby forefinger. Only Rufus couldn't pump with his feet because his legs were too short to reach the pedals. Jane or Joe had to pump for him.

They loved the organ. They played "Old Black Joe" over and over again. They took turns the whole afternoon. This pumping with your feet was a strange sort of business, they thought, but they had had good training, Joey on his bicycle and Jane on the sewing machine. Soon they were able to play "Old Black Joe" with both forefingers an octave apart. Now they really had music.

Rufus discovered two small round wooden trays that hinged to both ends of the organ beside the keys. They were covered with green felt.

"What are these for?" asked Rufus.

"For vases of flowers?" asked Jane.

"For lamps maybe," said Joe. They put the two smallest oil lamps on either side. What a sight that would be at Christmas time! The tree lighted, and the lamps on the organ lighted, and one of them seated at the organ, playing.

Then they carefully placed Mama's mandolin on top of the organ. And Rufus went digging among his things for his harmonica. When he found it he got up on the chair and put it beside the mandolin. A toy xylophone that had been in the family a long time completed the collection.

"There!" said Jane. "This is the music room. All we need now is sheets of music with the notes on them."

"I like better playing by ear," said Joe.

"Yes, I do, too," said Jane, "but it looks good to see music on the organ."

When Sylvie came home from choir rehearsal she was easily persuaded to put her precious sheets of music on the organ. Now everything was beautiful. Mama admired the music room and said, "Isn't it a pity I had to sell my lovely guitar?" Then she went into the kitchen to prepare the supper while Sylvie sat down to play.

Sylvie could play the organ with both hands and the hands played different parts. She also used all her fingers. She had practiced quite a lot on the piano in the parish house.

Jane sat in the big armchair, her legs flung over one of the arms. She was thinking yesterday they didn't have an organ and today they did, and the best thing to do with an organ was to give organ recitals. She wanted to give the organ recitals herself. "Seated one day at the organ," she hummed. That's what Sylvie was playing now. Sylvie was the best player of all the four Moffats. There was no doubt about it. Perhaps Sylvie was the one who should give the organ recitals. But when did Sylvie ever have time? Choir rehearsals, plays at the Town Hall, her dances, her friends, her diary, drawing! All these things took up Sylvie's time. She was hardly ever at home.

Maybe it would not take Janey long, a few days, say, to catch up with Sylvie and play as well as she. What Janey wanted in the organ recitals was loud notes, one running into the next, that would almost shake the house down. She did not want the drowsy kind that nearly put you to sleep, like the droning of insects on a hot afternoon.

Excitement over the organ continued for some days and it reached its peak the following Saturday. That was the day that Janey decided to

give her first organ recital. All during the week she had become more and more entranced with this idea. She decided to give the recital herself and she told no one about it, for she meant it to be a surprise to the rest of the family. She had first planned to give the organ recital on Sunday which would give her another day to practice, but when she heard that Mr. Julius Sampson was giving one himself that day at Woolsey Hall, she changed her day to Saturday. She would not wish to take away any of his audience. So Saturday was to be the day. Janey tried to keep the music thundering and crashing through her mind the way she remembered it had done at Woolsey Hall. The trouble was that whenever she tried to practice that way, Mama would call out from the kitchen, "Janey, play softly, please!"

But another real drawback was that Jane simply did not have the time to practice. Rufus and Joey were still just as eager to play the organ as she was and they all three wanted to play at the same time. Jane and Joe got tired of pumping for Rufus. However, he cleverly learned to play standing up, while pumping with one foot.

Rufus could always outwit his short legs. He had learned to ride Joey's bike by sticking one leg under the crossbar to the far pedal. The oldest inhabitant saw him riding this way one day and exclaimed, "My, what an extraordinary sense of balance this fellow has!"

Mama said Rufus would break the organ but Rufus loved playing so much he wouldn't stop.

So Saturday morning came without Janey having had a great deal of time at the organ. But whenever she thought of the way the music sounded in Woolsey Hall, she was confident it would sound as well in the Moffats' green and white parlor. She made a sign in large red crayon letters: "Organ Recital at two o'clock by *one of the Moffats*." She did not say by *Jane Moffat* because she thought that if she got scared she would persuade Rufus to play as he was such an odd sight, standing and pumping with one foot and playing "My Country, 'Tis of Thee." That is all Rufus could play, but he could play that like lightning. She nailed the sign to the porch.

"What does that say?" asked Rufus curiously.

"This says organ recital at two o clock," said Jane.

"Oh," said Rufus, not in the least surprised; "well, who's going to see that sign way back here?"

That's right, thought Jane, who could see it? The Moffats' house was set so far back from the street that no one passing by could see the sign. So she took it down and tied it to the large elm tree in front of their long green lawn. After this, Jane chased Rufus away from the organ for the rest of the morning so she could practice. She was firm about it.

"Rufus, go away," she said. "After the recital this afternoon you can have the organ for all the rest of the day."

However, she remembered she might need him; so she added, "But don't go far, you ought to be here for the recital 'cause I'm your sister."

She was a little disturbed to find that Joey had already gone on an all day hike out to the Sleeping Giant. And that Sylvie had planned to spend the day making paper flowers for the fair at the parish house. Goodness! She'd better see that Rufus stayed around in case she needed help. In the meanwhile she wished Mama would go somewhere for it was hard to make the kind of music that rocked the house with Mama saying all the time, "Oh, Jane, please! Don't make all that noise."

At last, however, Mama put on her hat and gloves and went to town to buy the week's provisions. Then Jane tried crashing the music out on the organ for all she was worth.

Rufus tore from the house bellowing, "Criminenty, Jane!" And he didn't come back until it was time for lunch.

"He really doesn't appreciate music," thought Jane. "But then, he's awfully little," she excused him.

To tell the truth though, Jane herself was far from satisfied with her playing. Even with no one around she could not get that swelling effect that she wanted. Also the right pedal had taken to giving a rasping gasp every time she brought her foot down on it. Feeling tired, Jane sat back and let the music thunder and swell only in her head. She decided not to practice any more, but to keep the music in her head this way and then just crash it out at two o'clock.

When Rufus came home for lunch she asked him to help her with the chairs.

"Who's coming?" he asked.

"Well, I don't know yet. But probably plenty of people will, with that sign out there."

Rufus helped Jane arrange the dining room chairs in a semi-circle. Then Jane picked some daisies in the lot across the street and these she put in tall jelly glasses on the small hinged trays at either end of the organ. Next she put on her best white piqué dress. She begged Rufus to put on a clean sailor suit. This he absolutely refused to do. Saturday was Saturday.

"Well, at least you can wash your face," begged Jane. Rufus did not want to do this either, but Jane caught him with the wash cloth and got the worst smudges off.

Now it was nearly two o'clock. She had been so busy she had not been thinking about the music. She hoped it would swell through the house in the proper way, banging against people's ear drums. She wondered if there would be chairs enough for the audience. Supposing hundreds came like at Woolsey Hall? If they did, they would have to sit on the long green lawn.

The idea of hundreds coming made Jane suck in her breath. Stage-struck! That's what she was, stage-struck.

She went to the window and lifted the curtain, hardly daring to look. Were the crowds arriving? No—nobody was coming. She should have made lots of signs and put them in store windows and on the bulletin board in front of the Town Hall. "Seated one day at the organ," she hummed.

Nobody was going to come, she thought. But as she was thinking this, she saw Clara Pringle and her little brother, Brud. Clara looked at the sign on the tree and then straggled up the walk, dragging Brud along. Brud looked as though he had been crying. Tears were in his eyes.

Jane met them at the door.

"We come to the show," said Clara.

"There isn't any show," said Jane. "This is goin' to be an organ recital."

"All right then," said Clara, "here's my pins."

She emptied a handful of pins into Janey's palm. In this neighborhood ten pins or one cent was the usual price of admission.

"Does he have to pay?" asked Clara, pointing to Brud, who was standing there looking very miserable.

"No," said Jane. "And neither do you. This is free. Like at Woolsey Hall. Did you ever have to pay to go there?" she asked scornfully, dropping the pins back into Clara's hand.

"Never been," said Clara.

Clara and Brud went into the parlor and sat down together in the big armchair. They squirmed around until they were comfortable and then pulled out their lollipops. Imagine bringing lollipops to an organ recital! thought Jane. Then

there was a shuffling step on the porch. My goodness, the oldest inhabitant! The most important
man in Cranbury! How nice of him to come!
Jane couldn't say one word. He sat down on a
corner of the couch and beamed. Jane closed the
window behind him so he wouldn't catch cold.

She looked at the clock in the kitchen and
found it was just two o'clock. Time to begin. She
went to the front window for one last look. It
was not good to begin until everyone was seated.
But Heavens! Who were all those people? Dozens of ladies, all dressed in white, gathered
around the big elm tree, talking, laughing and
screaming. "Look, girls," said one, pointing to
the sign, " 'Organ recital by one of the Moffats!' "

"Let's go, let's go," they chorused.

"Yes. We have plenty of time," said one.

Now the ladies in white were all coming up
the path. With their scarves fluttering in the
summer breeze they looked like butterflies. One
seemed to be Miss Buckle and one looked like
Mrs. Price, but Jane wasn't sure. With so many
ladies it was hard to tell.

Jane fled into the dining room, screaming
"Mama! Mama!"

But Mama had gone out again. Jane couldn't
even find Rufus. And of course Sylvie and Joe

had not yet returned. Only Catherine-the-cat was there on the window sill and she looked as though she were saying, "Now see what you've gotten yourself into."

"Oh, oh," groaned Jane, hearing the steps on the porch. She could flee, run out the back door, and pretend it was all a joke. But could she? No.

The honor of the Moffats forbade this. What would the oldest inhabitant think? He might never speak to her again. Besides how could she ever look Clara Pringle in the face again? She had said organ recital. So all right then, organ recital.

Jane opened the screen door. Miss Buckle—it was Miss Buckle—stepped in first.

"Hello, Jane," she said with a brisk smile, "we are the ladies of P'fessor Fairweather's Browning Society on our annual outing. We see there is an organ recital today. So—here we are."

To those behind her she said in the crisp way she had of talking, "This is Jane Moffat—the middle one."

"Oh!" said the ladies, the ones in back standing on tiptoe to get a look at Jane. "Well, is it time for the concert?"

"It's not a concert," said Jane, "it's an organ recital."

"I see," nodded the ladies. "Is it time for that then?"

Jane nodded her head slowly and the crowd came in. Jane thought to herself, "I should have had an usher."

The ladies arranged themselves around the room, on the porch, and some out on the lawn, sitting on their handkerchiefs to keep from getting grass stains. While they were so arranging themselves, the oldest inhabitant beamed and nodded his head. Brud Pringle watched him fascinated and offered him a lick of his lollipop.

Jane sat down to play.

Miss Buckle said, "Hush, girls," and everyone grew still.

Jane too remained silent and motionless. Perhaps she was dreaming. But a glance through her lashes out of the corner of her eye convinced her there really were lots and lots of ladies all over the place. Organ recital! Music! Bach! Words that no longer had any meaning for her raced through her head. She finally raised her hands to the keyboard. She began pumping hard and desperately with her feet, hoping it would be like Julius Sampson at Woolsey Hall when the first powerful notes shook the audience. However, she was not really one bit surprised when she recognized the first few notes as those of "My Country, 'Tis of Thee." Each note was accented by a breathless wheeze from the tired pedal.

The first few notes though were all anyone was destined to hear. For, as Janey pumped down on the pedals with might and main, they gave one loud gasp, and then with a plaintive, whish-

ing noise, like air going out of a rubber balloon, they slumped to the floor, exhausted, defeated by a week of Rufus' rapid one-foot pedaling, and by Janey's own passionate outbursts. Anyway, there they were, flat on the ground, and though Janey conscientiously dug at them with her toes to bring them up again, it was useless. They would not rise again. To tell the truth, Jane was really relieved. However, she was too embarrassed to turn around.

"It's broke," she murmured.

"Oh, what a pity," said Miss Buckle. "We shall . . ." But what Miss Buckle was going to say, no one ever knew. All of a sudden from out of the open places over the sunken pedals fluttered a horde of moths. They had been hatching for some time in the felt linings within the organ, and now they all took flight. There seemed to be thousands of them. The ladies screamed. They covered their ears and held onto their heads, while the moths fluttered blindly about. The oldest inhabitant just sat and beamed, blowing them out of his whiskers now and then. Brud Pringle tottered around the room trying to catch them in his sticky hands. Catherine-the-cat with a gleam in her eye leapt from chair to table pursuing the fluttering moths. Jane didn't know what to do. She wished she had a butterfly net.

"Oh, oh, oh! Run, girls, run!" screamed one of the ladies and they all made for the door, with moths settling on their hair-nets and even getting down their necks. "Save me!" cried Mrs. Price, banging through the screen door. And all the ladies rushed from the house, followed by a stream of the fluttering moths. Fortunately Mama was coming up the walk.

"What's going on?" she asked in amazement.

Without waiting for an answer she tried to restore order.

"Shoo! Shoo!" She waved her gloves at the moths. Some of the ladies helped by swishing their scarves but most of them ran around in circles, fingers in their ears and eyes tightly closed. Mrs. Price ran and hid in the honeysuckle bush. Jane shooed the moths off the oldest inhabitant although he said not to bother. He didn't mind them. They didn't bite.

Gradually, the moths disappeared. Mrs. Price hesitantly emerged from the honeysuckle bush. But every now and then one of the insects would fly out of somebody's sleeve or scarf and there would be more squeals and screams.

"Now," said Mama when she learned what had happened, "everybody sit down quietly and we'll have some home-made grape juice." She didn't like to have people flee from her house. She thought grape juice would make up for it. The ladies sat down. They shook their clothes and they patted their hair. Then suddenly they all began to laugh. They screamed and shrieked now with laughter. Jane had heard ladies laugh like this when she went past a house where there was a party. It had never happened before at the Moffats' house though. Tears rolled down Miss Buckle's chubby cheeks. Even Mrs. Price smiled wanly.

While they were sipping their grape juice and laughing merrily, Rufus rode up on his scooter. A party! When Jane told him about the moths, he was sorry he hadn't been there. He might have collected enough to make his own exhibit case of them for nature study.

The oldest inhabitant was the first to leave. He looked all right still and none the worse for the experience, thought Jane.

"Thank you, mysterious middle Moffat," he said to her as he shuffled down the path. "It was really better than pulling rabbits out of sleeves."

Jane smiled at him. Mysterious or middle or both, she and he were still friends. That was good.

The Pringles left next, covered with ginger-snap crumbs. And when all the ladies of the Browning Society finally fluttered down the path with a few last moths hovering behind them, Jane sat down on the top step of the porch munching a ginger-snap. If she wanted to give any organ recitals, she thought, she would have to study and study and study and study. Otherwise, all that would come out when she sat down to play would be "My Country, 'Tis of Thee" with two fingers at the most, and you couldn't hope to shake people out of their seats with that.

Unless, of course, the organ was full of moths, like this one.

3

BEST FRIENDS

"Wait for me!" Nancy had said to Jane when they parted after school. "I have to practice for an hour. Then we'll play."

Jane didn't know what they were going to do, play in Nancy's gymnasium in the attic, paint paper dolls, or play hide-and-go-seek with Nancy's sister, Beatrice. They often played with Beatrice even though she was a year younger, and only in

Room Four. Now, Jane was sitting here on the back fence waiting for Nancy to finish her practicing and whistle for her.

A long high whistle and a shorter low note. That's the way Nancy whistled for her. She whistled this way in the morning when it was time to go to school, and at noon when it was time to go back. They always went to school together and they came home together, too, both at noontime and in the afternoon. They did their home work together. For instance, if the teacher said, "Find out something about the artist, Millet, when he was born, when he died, and what else he painted besides this picture on the classroom wall called, 'The Gleaners'," they studied the encyclopedia together.

Best friends! That's what that was.

The first time that Jane saw Nancy was the day the Moffats moved into this little house. That very day Nancy said to Janey that very likely they would be best friends. She didn't even know Janey; she just must have liked her looks. The next day Nancy and her family had gone away to Maine on their vacation and Jane did not see her again until the first day of school.

This year Jane was going to a different school. She had looked around the room to see who was in the class. She knew some of the children for they were from the school she used to go to; but some of them she didn't know as well, for they had always come to this school. Nancy Stokes was one of these.

She must have come home in the middle of the night because Jane had watched and watched for her yesterday and by bed-time she had not come home yet.

Naturally Jane did not stare across the room at her. Nancy had been away for a long time. She might have forgotten Jane or she might have found a new best friend. But when the class was standing in line in the hall, legs moving up and down in time to the music the teacher was playing on the victrola, Jane found that Nancy was her marching partner.

The children must not look to the left or the right. Eyes straight ahead! Shoulders back! That's the way they had to stand. The teacher was standing at the head of the line, with her head bobbing up and down, clapping her hands and marching her legs in time to the music too. The class had to march a long time, legs going up and down in the same spot, before the teacher said, "March!"

"Practice," thought Jane. If they were prop-

erly wound up before starting, no one could get out of step.

While they were warming up this way, eyes straight ahead, shoulders back, legs going up and down, Nancy whispered to Jane:

"Aren't you that girl in the house in back of ours?"

"Yes," whispered Jane.

"We'll walk home together. Wait for me," said Nancy.

"Yes."

Jane smiled to herself. This girl remembered her! Out of all the people in the class, and it was a big one, she remembered who Janey was. Of course it was easy for Jane to remember Nancy because Nancy had golden curls. "Aren't you that girl?" she repeated to herself.

That had been the first day they had walked home from school together. And they had every day since. When they got home, "So long!" Nancy would yell, and Jane would climb over the high board fence into her own yard.

Nancy's mother said they would wear all her nice green paint off the fence, so after a few days she had her handy man take out the corner board and put hinges on it. Now they had a real little swinging door to step through. And they weren't spoiling the looks.

Janey banged her feet against the fence, her side of the fence, where there wasn't any paint. She did wish Nancy would come now. And she wished that Nancy did not have to practice her music so much. Then they could play together all the time. But just then Nancy did come to her door and she whistled, a long high note and a short low one.

"Jan-ey!" she called for good measure.

Jane jumped into the Stokes' yard and ran through the apple orchard. She went into the Stokes' big house. Now she was able to walk in Nancy Stokes' house all right, but she remembered the first time she had come here. That time when she had stepped into this house, she had nearly fallen down. What was this floor made of? Glass? That's what she had first thought. But it wasn't; it was just a very shiny floor. And the rugs! Jane thought she was stepping on moss, the kind that grew around the brooks in the woods. They were real rugs, though, not moss. Mama said there were a lot of houses in New York where she came from like that.

Now, of course, after many visits in this house,

Jane was able to walk on these floors. She never did really fall down. She slipped sometimes, but she didn't actually fall. It was lucky the oldest

inhabitant did not live in a house with floors of this sort, thought Jane. He would never reach the age of one hundred if he had to slide around like this.

Jane never ran through this house the way she did the Moffats' house. She just walked, and she walked the way she did on ice. She put her whole foot down and she took careful steps. Nancy and her sister ran through the house sometimes, and the rugs slid together in a heap behind them. They never fell down. They were used to the shiny floors. But so far, Jane had not tried running.

Now she carefully followed Nancy through the hall. "What'll we play?" asked Nancy. "Trapeze? Paper dolls?"

"Let's make paper dolls," suggested Jane.

So they went upstairs to Nancy's room. Going up the stairs was the hardest for they were the shiniest of all. Nancy just walked up and down without even hanging onto the banister, but Jane still had to hold on. She wished she could walk up and down the stairs the way Nancy did, just as easy as though they were the old ones at school, worn hollow in the middle from so many children stepping on them.

But then, Nancy was very brave. She wouldn't be afraid of shiny stairs. She was not afraid of one thing that Janey knew about so far. She got into fights with anybody that would pick on a smaller child, boys and girls alike. Jane wished she could be as brave as that.

If anyone asked Jane, "What kind of a girl is

Nancy? Describe her!" she would say, "This girl is brave, fearless, and kind to animals. She has golden curls and she laughs good."

Janey and Nancy sat down at Nancy's desk. They started to cut out paper dolls. Nancy made a horse for the prince to sit on. She did love animals. That's why she was so kind to them.

If Nancy ever saw a stray dog loping along the street in the sleet or in the rain, covered with mud, hungry, and thirsty, she'd take it home and bathe it in the Stokes' own white bath tub. That is, if Mrs. Stokes were away. Mrs. Stokes thought the set tubs in the cellar the place to bathe stray dogs, but Nancy thought the best was what all dogs deserved. That was the way she was about animals. After the bath she would give the dog a good dinner and keep him until the owner could be found. Then she would have to send the dog home. That always made her cry, having to send the dog home. Mrs. Stokes said the dogs weren't lost anyway, they knew where they were, and Nancy should not bring all these dogs home. But Nancy didn't think so. They were muddy and hungry and needed care, she said. Nancy also carried carrots and apples around in her pocket for any horse she might meet. Jane had read about people doing this in books, but she'd never known anyone like that in real life.

"Goodness!" said Nancy, bursting into a laugh as she held up her paper-doll horse. "Look at this horse, will you? What's the matter with him?"

"He slopes," said Jane.

Nancy laughed explosively again. Mrs. Stokes

came in from her room with a bit of darning in her hands.

"Nancy dear, please don't laugh so boisterously. Janey doesn't laugh that way. Try and laugh gently, the way Janey does."

Jane wiggled her toes in her shoes, embarrassed. This was a funny thing, she thought. Nancy's mother doesn't like the way Nancy laughs, but I do. Ha-ha! Like a firecracker. She herself was trying to learn to laugh the way Nancy laughed. She had practiced often, but so far she had not succeeded. Nancy's laugh was so hearty. It burst out suddenly in loud high notes and raced rapidly down the scale to a deep low pitch. Jane's laugh was more of an inside job. She shook silently and tears rolled down her cheeks. How could people tell whether she was laughing or crying, she wondered.

But when she tried laughing like Nancy, the effect was even worse. She always hoped it would sound like Nancy but it didn't. It sounded like herself, Jane, reading out loud in school. She would come upon the words, ha-ha, in the book. Should she say them the way they were written or should she laugh them? She always said them, ha-ha, like words, instead of like laughs.

Once they were reading a good book. The

teacher said, "Who can read this book with expression?" Janey raised her hand because she
had been reading to
herself with the most
wonderful expression.
But when she read out
loud, the teacher said,
"Goodness! Do you call
that expression?" And
Janey sat down. The
passage had had the
words ha-ha in it. Janey
thought perhaps the
teacher expected her
to laugh these words
instead of saying them.
But then the teacher
read out loud and when
she reached the words
ha-ha, she just said them too. She didn't laugh
them. So that couldn't be what was wrong with
Jane's expression.

Jane watched Nancy paint the paper-doll horse.
Yes, she thought, there were two things she
wanted to do like Nancy. One was to be brave
the way she was, and the other was to laugh the
way she did. Of course, once she learned to laugh

that way she would have to be careful not to do so in front of Mrs. Stokes, because she didn't seem to like it.

"How's that?" Nancy asked, holding her horse up again.

"It's good," said Jane.

Mrs. Stokes came into Nancy's room again, looking for the scissors.

"Mother," Nancy said, "may Jane stay to dinner?"

Jane squirmed her toes around in her shoes again. Maybe Mrs. Stokes wouldn't want her to stay for dinner. She might not have bought enough dinner for an extra person. But how could she say no with Jane sitting right there? She wished Nancy had arranged this when she was not around.

However, Mrs. Stokes said "Of course" so cordially she must really want her to stay.

"And perhaps Janey will spend the evening with you because Father and I are going to the concert at Woolsey Hall," she added.

"I'll ask Mama," said Jane. And she ran home.

Mama said it was all right and Jane put on a clean guimpe under her suspender dress. She wondered how the other Moffats liked it when she went away to dinner. Just three of them and

Mama at the table. Jane remembered when Sylvie was away at Camp Lincoln it was very lonely. But then, when she, Janey, was at the Stokes' she was only over the back fence, no distance at all.

She climbed up on the back fence now to wait a little while, for it was not yet six o'clock. She was glad she was going to have dinner with the Stokes, and she hoped that they would have lamb chops. She hoped they would have lamb chops because she saw that Olga, the maid, was there today. The Stokes did not have a maid all the time. Just once in a while. Jane had been to dinner once when they had had lamb chops, but Olga had not been there. Another time when Olga had been there, they had not had lamb chops. They had had fish. Today Jane prayed there would be both lamb chops and Olga. Why? Because she wanted to show Mrs. Stokes she knew a lot about manners.

Mama had taught all the Moffats a lot about manners. For instance, always let the older people speak first. Jane did that. Also, if you were having dinner in a house where there was a maid, and there were lamb chops for dinner, you should not accept a second lamb chop if it were the last one left on the platter after everybody had had one. Because that chop was for the maid and if you took it and ate it, the maid would have none.

So far this had not happened to Jane. She did hope that tonight they would have lamb chops so she could show them she knew about not eating the last chop.

The way Mama had found out about the last lamb chop was this. When she was about the size of Jane, she was visiting a friend in the Berkshires. In this house there was a maid. One night there were lamb chops for dinner. Everybody had a chop and ate it. On the platter there was one chop left. Everybody was offered this chop and refused. Then it was offered to Mama. Mama was still hungry, for the Berkshires make you very hungry. So she had accepted the chop and had eaten it.

Afterwards her friend's mother had told her that when there is one chop left on the plate, it is for the maid. Otherwise what would the maid have to eat? Didn't Mama want the maid to have a lamb chop too? Naturally, Mama felt very badly. So she had always told all her four children never to eat the last lamb chop if there were a maid in the kitchen.

Olga was there tonight, in the Stokes' kitchen.

Jane could see her head in the little window over the kitchen sink. Well, Olga needn't worry. Janey was coming to dinner. But Jane would not eat Olga's chop.

The six o'clock whistle blew. Janey jumped off the fence. She went into the Stokes' house. If only they had chops!

Everybody sat down around the shiny round table in the dining room. Mrs. Stokes sat opposite Mr. Stokes. Beatrice sat on one side. And Nancy and Jane, best friends, sat on the other side.

First they had vegetable soup. They ate this all right. There probably was a big kettle of soup on the stove, plenty for Olga and everybody. Even so, when Mrs. Stokes asked Jane if she would like some more soup, she said, "No, thank you," because she knew the real dinner had not commenced yet. When there was vegetable soup at home, the Moffats always had a second plateful, because there the vegetable soup was the real dinner.

So then Olga brought in the warm dinner plates. And next she brought in a steaming platter. She stood beside Mrs. Stokes to serve her first. Of course Jane did not look at the platter immediately lest she give the impression that she was greedy or too hungry. After a second or two she permitted her eyes to fall upon the platter. Oh, I do hope it's lamb chops, she thought.

It was lamb chops!

Olga and lamb chops!

Both!

However, Janey's first feeling of pleasure gave way immediately to one of perplexity.

There were only five chops on the platter. The four Stokes and Olga made five. And she made six. If this were like the time Mama ate the second lamb chop in the Berkshires, there should be six chops on the platter.

But there were only five. Of course four of them were for the four Stokes. That would leave just one on the platter. Should she take it or leave it for Olga? Mrs. Stokes had taken hers and now there were four. Olga moved around the table and stood beside Beatrice.

When Mama took the last chop that time, she had already eaten one. Now Jane had not eaten one so far. Goodness! What was she going to do? Beatrice helped herself to one without batting

an eyelash. Maybe Mr. Stokes does not like chops, thought Jane as Olga moved around to his side of the table. But this was not the case. He took his chop without any urging from anybody. And that left two chops. Nancy quickly helped herself to one of these, and then Olga stood beside Jane with the big platter, all empty now except for one big juicy lamb chop.

For her? Or for Olga?

Olga stood there. Janey glued her eyes on the chop. All the four Stokes sat with their hands in their laps while Janey thought. For her? Or for Olga?

If she took the chop and ate it, Mrs. Stokes might say to her, the way Mama's friend had when she was little, "When there is only one chop on the plate, it is for the maid."

But then Mama had already had one.

She and Olga might divide this one. Share and share alike, the way the Moffats did. But it is hard to cut a lamb chop in two.

Everybody was very quiet. They must be wondering what she was going to do. She wished she knew. Perhaps Olga had kept hers in the kitchen. Maybe she wasn't going to take any chances with a girl like Janey, thinking she might be like Mama in the Berkshires and eat two.

She wished she could say right out, "Is this my chop or Olga's?"

Pooh! Of course this was her chop, and she reached her hand towards the platter. . . . But then . . . and she drew her hand back . . . maybe this was a test of her manners. That thought persisted.

But wait . . . here was another thought. If Nancy came to dinner in the Moffats' house, of course they would make sure she had a chop. It was different in the Moffats' house though. There

they would all be sitting around the kitchen table ... too cold in the dining room ... and everybody could see at a glance exactly how many chops there were in the house. Moreover there wasn't any Olga to think about. But the way the Moffats would feel would be this: "Let the best chop be for Nancy, because she is company."

Why, that's what Janey was! Company! If she was company, she should have a chop. All right, then. She reached for the fork and at the same time Mrs. Stokes spoke.

She said, "Olga, I don't know what kind of manners Janey will think we have. Not to serve Janey her chop before Nancy and Beatrice! I am ashamed of you, Olga. You must remember always to serve the company first."

"Yes, Mrs. Stokes," said Olga.

Jane heaved a sigh of relief. Her chop. Those were Mrs. Stokes' own words. Jane took her chop.

"Oh, that's all right," said Jane. "I knew it was for me," and she smiled graciously at Olga to show her that her feelings had not been hurt at all by being served last.

Then everybody ate their dinner and talked and laughed; and they had chocolate pudding for dessert.

After dinner was over Nancy's mother and father had to hurry to the city to get to the concert on time. Jane went into the kitchen for a glass of water. There was Olga, eating her dinner. She had a nice juicy chop of her own! Phew! thought Jane. It certainly was lucky I knew enough manners to take that chop.

When she got home she told Mama that in the Stokes' house, when they had a maid and lamb chops, they did not put the maid's chop on the table at all. Every chop on the table was supposed to be for the people at the table. This was different from the Berkshires.

"And much more sensible," said Mama. "Why dangle a chop in front of somebody's nose, if it is not to be eaten?"

4

AN AFTERNOON WITH
THE OLDEST INHABITANT

Jane took the short cut across the huge, empty
lot to the library. She was in a hurry because
she had just gotten the idea that it would be fine
to read every book in the library. Of course not
all at once; just one at a time. She arrived there
hot and panting. The best way to go about reading every book in the library, she thought, was

to go to a certain section, take down the first book on the first shelf, get it stamped, take it home, read it, bring it back, and take out the very next book. In this way she would not miss one single book. She tiptoed over to one of the sections, took down the first book without looking to see what it was, and had it stamped at the desk. As she was about to leave she noticed Mr. Buckle in an armchair by the window.

"What book did you take, mysterious middle Moffat?" he asked her.

Jane showed him her book. She saw for the first time it was called "The Story of Lumber."

"H-m-m-m, 'The Story of Lumber' ... very mystifying," he said, and he put his forefinger on the side of his nose like Hawkshaw, the detective.

Jane played her part, too; then she backed out on tiptoes, waving a reassuring good-by to Miss Lamb, the librarian, who watched her with a truly mystified expression.

Jane read "The Story of Lumber" as rapidly as possible. It was not very interesting. But if she were going to read every book in the library, she would have to take the bad along with the good. She brought "The Story of Lumber" back the next day and took the next book. The oldest

inhabitant was sitting in the same place by the window. His soft white hair shone in the sunshine.

Again Jane showed him the new book she had borrowed and saw with a trace of dismay that this one was called "The Story of Cotton."

" 'The Story of Cotton' ... more mystifying than ever," whispered Mr. Buckle.

Jane played Hawkshaw a trifle absent-mindedly. She sat down on the granite steps outside the library and read for a while. This book also was far from interesting. Evidently she had chosen the wrong section to begin on. Where were all the books like "Heidi"? Still if she read the bad ones first, the good ones would be like dessert.

When she brought back "The Story of Cotton" and saw that the next book was "The Story of Sugar," she decided to try something different. She still planned to read every book in the library but she would take the best ones first. Then, by the time she finished all the good ones, she would be such a good reader she could just tear through things like "The Story of Sugar" in a few minutes.

She chose a bound volume of *St. Nicholas* magazine. This was full of good things. As she left the library she met Mr. Buckle coming up the granite steps. He was supporting himself by means of the brass railing.

"Hello, Mr. Buckle," said Jane. "I am going to read every book in the library," she added, feeling exuberant again now that she had something good.

Mr. Buckle nodded his head up and down, beaming. He was out of breath and he was hanging onto the brass railing.

"Is it cheating," Jane demanded, "if I don't

read every word in this big book? It's not really a book. It's a lot of magazines."

"Did you say to yourself, I am going to read every book and every magazine?"

"No . . . every book."

"Well, then, it's not cheating."

"But maybe a whole lot of magazines together makes a book."

"It is very mystifying," agreed Mr. Buckle, "but I think once a magazine, always a magazine."

Jane ran home the long way so she could race the trolley car to Ashbellows Place. She was a good runner and almost always beat the trolley to her corner. Running around to the back yard and climbing onto the high board fence, she peered through the apple trees. She hoped that Nancy Stokes would have come home from her piano lesson by now. But Nancy was nowhere in sight. She must have had to go somewhere with her mother.

So Jane went around front and sat down on the little square porch to read her *St. Nicholas*. The first story began, "In the middle of the night . . ."

In the middle of the night . . . It reminded Jane of her own position in the Moffat family. It was now definitely established that she was the middle Moffat. Mama introduced her as "Jane,

the middle Moffat" not only to the Gillespie girls but also to the new curate of the church for whom she was making vestments and cassocks.

Of course the only person to whom she had made that mistake about being the mysterious middle Moffat was Mr. Buckle. And, as it turned out, this had not proved to be such a grave error anyway. In fact, he seemed to enjoy the game of Hawkshaw, the detective, very much. And if he liked it, and he was the oldest inhabitant and the most important person in the town, it certainly had not done any harm, this calling herself the mysterious middle Moffat. It might even, by keeping him in such good spirits, help him live to be one hundred.

Jane was doing all she could about that. For instance, she sometimes followed him from a distance to see that he crossed the street safely and that no dogs jumped out at him unexpectedly and made him lose his balance. Whenever she heard of a new family moving to Cranbury, she checked up immediately to find out how old the oldest person in that family was. When she found that there was no one ninety-nine or over, she quickly told Mr. Buckle so he would know he was still the oldest inhabitant in town.

Janey tried to be near by whenever the oldest inhabitant was shuffling past the firehouse, because the Cranbury fire alarm was the loudest in the whole state. What a blast when it went off! And it was so sudden! There was no warning at all. Jane always said politely when she joined him here, "Don't we have the loudest fire alarm here in Cranbury?" This was just to remind him to be on guard and steel himself in case it blew.

Yes, she was doing everything she could to help him reach one hundred. Just this afternoon running home from the library, she had kicked aside a fallen branch, a broken bottle, an orange peel, so the way would be clear when Mr. Buckle

came home. She even occasionally carried around an old umbrella so that he would not get caught in the rain. Of course she could not spend her whole time this way, but she did as much as she could.

Once she had seen Mr. Buckle go out and she

had followed at a distance with the Moffats' big old umbrella. She really thought it might rain because the sparrows were chattering in the big elm tree in front of the house. Somebody told her once this was a sure sign of rain. When she reached the Green, there he was blowing cotton to the birds. Puffs of cotton on the grass looked like dandelions gone to seed.

Just as Janey arrived, the sky actually, all of a sudden, did turn black all over. The rain came marching up the street. She reached the oldest inhabitant and opened the umbrella over his head just as the big drops started to fall on his side of the street.

"This is very mysterious," he said, "your being on hand with the umbrella." And they had walked home together in the rain.

Now, while Jane was rocking back and forth in the green rocker, and reading her *St. Nicholas* magazine, a fog began to roll in from the Sound. Jane looked up from her book. A fog! And it seemed to be growing thicker and thicker. She put her book down and watched it roll in. Soon she could hardly see the lot across the street. This was going to be a really heavy fog, perhaps as good a fog as they had in London.

She ran down the steps and up and down the

Moffats' long lawn trying to separate the fog, as though it were a gauzy curtain. Then she could see what was going on in the world. As she reached the sidewalk, she slipped on some damp autumn leaves and ran into Miss Buckle, the daughter of the oldest inhabitant, who caught her in her arms.

"Goodness, Jane. What a start you gave me. I'm afraid I'm going to be late to P'fessor Fairweather's Browning Society. . . . Good-by, child."

And she set Jane firmly on the walk. Jane watched the oldest inhabitant's daughter disappear in the fog. P'fessor Fairweather . . . Jane liked the way she said that. She never said *Pro*fessor Fairweather. Just P'fessor Fairweather, very fast. That was nice, the way she talked. Everything she said sounded so important.

Well! Miss Buckle was going to the Browning Society, leaving the oldest inhabitant all alone. Jane hoped he had gotten home from the library in the fog safely. Supposing some witch who was exactly one hundred was jealous of him and had snatched him down under the squash vines that grew so thickly all over one corner of the lot. That's the way it might be if this were a fairy tale and not Ashbellows Place. However, fairy tale or not, she decided to spend the after-

noon with the old-
est inhabitant so
he would not be
tempted to go out
in the fog.

Once the oldest
inhabitant had said
to her:

"Come in and see
my chicken-bone
furniture some
day."

Today would be a good chance to do this. Of
course she would not say she had come to call
on him to keep him from getting lost in the
fog. But she would say she had come to see
his chicken-bone furniture. Besides she really
owed him a visit since he had come to her organ
recital.

Jane ran into her house to get her knitting, for
she intended to stay with the oldest inhabitant
until the fog lifted. Then she marched up the
street and onto Mr. Buckle's porch. She walked
right in. She tiptoed through the little parlor
with the black horse-hair chairs and sofa, and
she went into the sitting-room, where the oldest
inhabitant was bent over a big book. He bal-

anced it halfway on his knees and halfway on the little oval-shaped table beside him.

"Hello, Mr. Buckle," said Jane politely.

"Hello, Jane," said the oldest inhabitant.

"I've come to see the bones," said Jane.

"Ah, yes," said the oldest inhabitant. "The chicken-bone furniture . . ."

Jane glanced around the room. She had never been in this house before. On one wall was a picture of the ruins of Pompeii, and on another was a picture of a lot of sheep huddled together in a blizzard. There was a picture exactly like this in Nancy's house. Jane preferred colored pictures such as the one the Moffats had in their green and white parlor of a milkmaid leading home the cows.

The oldest inhabitant showed her a little glass cabinet in a corner of the room. This held the furniture he had carved out of chicken bones. Jane stood with her hands behind her back so Mr. Buckle would not think she would touch things and break them. She looked at the chicken-bone furniture in amazement. What lovely little things! Tiny tables, chairs, cupboards, beds, a sofa, a bookcase with what looked like real little books, and even the tiniest of clocks!

"Oh, how nice!" exclaimed Jane.

"Yes ... those are all carved out of chicken bones. Every piece. I did them all by hand."

"My," said Jane. "What a lot of chickens you must have eaten!"

"Yes ..." said the oldest inhabitant. "They are very famous. Peabody Museum is asking for them all the time. My daughter frequently suggests that I give them to the Museum, but I like to keep them here."

Jane admired the chicken-bone furniture for quite some while. The oldest inhabitant sat down in his little rocking chair again. Now that Jane had seen the chicken-bone furniture, she wondered if the oldest inhabitant expected her to go home. He had gone home after the organ recital. But first they had had cookies and grape juice. He might think if she stayed longer that she wanted something to eat. But she had resolved to stay until the fog lifted or Miss Buckle came home. However, she couldn't look at the chicken-bone furniture the whole afternoon. And he might get alarmed if she sat down and took out her knitting. He might think, "Goodness! Is she going to stay all day?"

That's what the Moffats always thought when Mrs. Price arrived and sat down with her knitting. For she usually did spend the entire afternoon there, while everybody was wanting to do something else.

Fortunately the oldest inhabitant spoke just then and relieved Jane of her embarrassment. "Well, middle Moffat. Now we have seen the chicken-bone furniture. How would you like to look at pictures through the stereoscope?"

"That would be nice," agreed Jane.

The oldest inhabitant went to a little closet in the corner and came back with a pile of pictures and the stereoscope. He put the pile of pictures on the table beside him and sat down. Jane pulled up a chair.

"Now you fit the pictures in and we'll look," said Mr. Buckle.

So Jane fitted a picture in the stereoscope and passed it to the oldest inhabitant, who adjusted it to his eyes. He peered at it with his white head thrust a little forward. Then he handed it to Jane and she adjusted it to her eyes. One by one they went through all the pictures this way. When it was Jane's turn to look, she never knew exactly how long she should look. She didn't want to look too long and make the oldest inhabitant tired of waiting for the next picture. And she didn't want to look too little and give the impression she was not appreciating the beauty of the scene. At length she decided to count up to ten, slowly. There! That was a good polite time to look at each one, she thought.

It really was funny how these two same pictures on the cards jumped together into one picture when you looked at them through the stereoscope. In real life they looked like picture post cards with two identical pictures separated by a line down the middle. But through the stereoscope the two pictures hopped together into one.

How the man, walking along the woody path, suddenly jumped out at you! A real man in a

straw hat! The mountains stood out from one another, and the waterfall looked as though it might splash you. A castle hidden in the trees suddenly emerged. You could almost pick the flowers, especially the edelweiss! There was a nearness and a farness to the pictures, as though you were standing on the top of Shingle Hill and looking at real scenery. But of course these scenes were of the Alps, not Shingle Hill. One picture showed an old Swiss with a long white beard sitting in front of his mountain cottage. Goats were nibbling the grass.

"Maybe the alms-uncle in 'Heidi,' " thought Jane.

"Another oldest inhabitant," said Mr. Buckle, laughing.

Jane smiled at him and looked a longer time, counting up to fifteen at this one.

When they had finished looking at the pictures, the oldest inhabitant said, "I see you have brought your knitting."

"Yes," said Jane. "A scarf for the soldiers in France."

She held it up for him to see. She wished she could knit red rows and blue rows for a change. Maybe she could change it into a helmet. It was not long enough for a scarf yet, but it was nearly long enough for a helmet.

"Would you change this into a helmet?" she asked the oldest inhabitant.

"It's supposed to be a scarf?"

"Yes."

"My goodness! Changing scarves into helmets! The mysterious middle Moffat!" exclaimed the oldest inhabitant.

Jane laughed, and whoops! she lost a stitch!

"Catch it! Catch it!" shouted the oldest inhabitant as though it were a runaway horse.

Jane sat down and clumsily recaptured the stitch.

"Narrow escape," said Mr. Buckle.

"My goodness," thought Jane. "He shouldn't shout like that. I better not drop any more stitches."

She knit one or two rows in silence. The oldest inhabitant watched her for a while and then he bent his head over his book. All you could hear now in the house was the sound of Janey's knitting needles clicking together, the soft breathing of the oldest inhabitant, and the tick-tock of the comfortable clock on the mantel. Mr. Buckle breathed in to the clock's tick and out to the clock's tock.

Jane knit and the clock tick-tocked. The quiet made her sleepy. She heard coal being dumped into Clara Pringle's cellar. Bag after bag rattled down the chute. What a lot of bags of coal they were getting, good hard black coal! Must be enough for a year at least. In the Moffats' house they never had more than one bag of coal at a time ... She heard an occasional horse and wagon joggle by. Clop, clop. And she heard Joey call, "Ru-fus! Mama wants you to come home." All these noises sounded miles away.

Jane thought she would like to stretch her legs now and look out of the window, and see if she could see any of these things that were going on out there in the fog. But of course she did not do this. The oldest inhabitant might get it into his head that she did not like sitting here, or that he should offer her something to eat.

She looked at the oldest inhabitant to see if he had gone to sleep. But he hadn't, and he surprised her very much by saying, "How about a good game of double solitaire now?"

Double solitaire! Her favorite game! She and Joey and Rufus played it all the time. She nodded her head up and down. She would play slowly and let him win, she thought. She was the quickest double solitaire player of the Moffats. That was one thing, like running, that she was very good at. It made Rufus mad, she went so fast. She would be careful and not go too fast for the oldest inhabitant.

Mr. Buckle pushed aside the lamp, a small plaster model of the Yale Bowl, a copy of the *National Geographic*, and the red-fringed tablecloth. This table had a white marble top, wonderful for games! He pulled out a little drawer that was ordinarily hidden by the tablecloth and took out two decks of playing cards. Jane pulled her chair around opposite him, and they were ready to begin.

He gave her one deck of cards. "Shuffle!" he bade her.

Jane separated her pack of cards into two piles and shuffled one into the other. The oldest inhabitant did not like the way she shuffled.

"That is not the way to shuffle," he said. "This is the way to shuffle."

And he held the pack in his left hand, took some of the cards out with his right hand, and shuffled them back and forth so fast you couldn't see them. He was the fastest shuffler Jane had ever known.

"There," he said. "Now! We are ready to begin."

They laid out the cards neatly for the game and all was ready.

"Start!"

The oldest inhabitant bit out the words like a sergeant giving a command.

Start! The cards flew! Slap down the ace of hearts! Who would get the two on first? The oldest inhabitant! Slap on the three . . . the four. Ace of spades! Slap down the two . . . the three. Who'd get the four on first?

The oldest inhabitant!

He flipped the cards through the air between

plays! The cards were flying! Slap on the jack
... the queen ... the king! Look at the dia-
monds! Build up the diamond pile. Who had the
seven?

Janey!

Put it on quick. Down with the eight ... the
nine. The oldest inhabitant got his card there
first almost every time. When he didn't, he put
the card on the edge of the table, flipped it
lightly in the air, making it turn a somersault,
caught it neatly between thumb and forefinger,
and returned it to its proper place while Jane
was racing for the next card. Flying through the
air, aces, spades, hearts, twos, threes, jacks,
queens, everything!

Jane's head spun! Her eyes felt crossed. She
played faster than she had ever played in her
whole life in order to uphold the honor of the
Moffats. Let the oldest inhabitant win! Pooh!
Not to be licked hollow the way she licked Clara
Pringle, that's all she hoped for now.

The oldest inhabitant was winning! And not
because she was letting him either. Letting him!
What a foolish thought! The oldest inhabitant, a
veteran of the Civil War, who sat on the review-
ing stand for every important occasion, and gave
out the diplomas at graduation ... soon to be

one hundred years old. . . . What had she been thinking? Letting him win! Of course a man such as this would win.

Mr. Buckle flipped his last card, the king of hearts, into the air. It turned a neat somersault right smack down on the heart pile.

The oldest inhabitant had won!

"There!" he beamed, rocking back and forth in his chair, his hands on his knees, watching while Jane finished up her last cards.

"Gee . . ." gasped Jane. "You're some player!"

"Shall we have another game?" he asked. "Or is it time for Nellie? She doesn't like me to play doubles."

And at that very moment the front door opened. The oldest inhabitant swept all the cards into the little drawer, yanked the tablecloth back into place, and the Yale Bowl, too! Just in time!

"Hello, Father. And, why, hello, Jane!" said Miss Buckle, bustling into the room, the cherries on her hat shaking and rattling together. "I declare . . . P'fessor Fairweather. . . . What an inspiration! My . . ."

Jane backed out of the room and out of the house, scarcely able to say good-by. Goodness! What a game! Her head was whirling and she still felt dizzy. She must practice that card trick.

The one in which you flipped the card off the edge of the table and caught it neatly between thumb and forefinger. That would impress Joey and Rufus, and Nancy Stokes, too.

"Watch me!" she'd say. And the cards would flip through the air the way they had for the oldest inhabitant.

5

THE MECHANICAL WIZARD

"See you later!" Jane yelled after Nancy who was disappearing through the apple trees. Nancy was going to take her music lesson.

Jane crawled through the little gate in the fence. When she stepped into her own back yard, she knew at once that something had happened, but she didn't know what. Oh, there it was! Smoke was coming out of the chimney of the new house next door. Curtains were in the window. Mops and brooms were on the back porch. People had moved in. Jane wondered who they were.

She ran around to the front yard. It was lucky that she and Joey and Rufus had picked up all the shavings and scraps of wood for kindling that were left over from building the house. Because of course now everything over there would belong to the new people.

Joey and Rufus were standing beside the honeysuckle bush peering into the yard next door. Jane went up to the bush and peered in too. There was a motorcycle in the next yard, upside down. Maybe a motorcycle policeman had moved in.

"Who moved in?" she asked.

"Wallie Bangs," Joe answered enthusiastically.

"Who's Wallie Bangs?" asked Jane.

"You don't know who Wallie Bangs is? He's the mechanical genius. Everybody knows him. He's a wiz. Whole school talks about him," said Joe.

"And he lives here now?" Jane was impressed. A genius. It seemed almost unbelievable that not only the oldest inhabitant but also the mechanical genius should live on Ashbellows Place.

"Sure," said Rufus. "See that motorcycle? He's been making it go the whole afternoon."

"You mean he rides it in and out?"

"No," said Joe. "He just makes the motor go while it's upside down. He's fixin' it. Takes it apart and puts it together again. But it isn't right yet. He has to work hard."

"Is that what a mechanical genius does?"

"Yeh. He takes things apart," said Joe. "He's got Clara Pringle's skates and my dollar watch too. He takes them all apart."

"Has he got any brothers and sisters?"

"Yeh. One brother. In Room Six."

"Is his brother a mechanical genius too?"

"No, he's just a fella."

"Oh ..." Jane wished she had something for the mechanical genius to take apart. Things probably ran twice as fast after he'd taken them apart.

"Here he comes!" said Joe. And Rufus and Janey stared hard.

A big boy who wore long pants came marching around the new house next door into the back yard. His step was sure and purposeful. He had lots of skates in one hand, swinging them like a catch of fish. He had a battery in the other hand and what looked like a great many clocks under his arm. He disappeared into the cellar with all these things.

"He has a wonderful workshop down there, I bet," whispered Joe.

Then the boy, it *was* Wallie Bangs, came up into the air again and he marched over to the upside-down motorcycle. He stood beside it a moment, surveying it, his forefinger crooked on his chin and a frown on his brow. He then proceeded to pull plugs, push valves, slap the machine here and there, and all of a sudden a series of loud putt-putt-putt explosions rent the air.

This appeared to delight the boy. He kept making the explosions happen and he listened with his head cocked to one side. Now its putt-putts

began to sound the way a motorcycle sounds when it is tearing through the countryside at high speed.

"Maybe he will turn it right side up and ride it now," Jane whispered.

But he didn't. The motorcycle kept roaring away as though it were speeding along the highway but all the while it was just there, upside down in the yard next door. Jane and Joey and Rufus stared, fascinated. They couldn't help jumping every time the big Fuff! happened.

"When he gets that motorcycle fixed, he's gonna fix all those clocks and things he's got down there in the cellar," marveled Rufus.

All of a sudden between the sput-sputs, Wallie Bangs spoke.

"You kids got anything you want fixed?" he asked without looking up. The Moffats were surprised. They jumped for they didn't even know he knew they were there.

"You've got my watch," said Joe.

"Oh, have I?" said Wallie carelessly. "Well, any clocks, skates ... anything mechanical ..." And then he forgot he was talking and made his motorcycle give out some more good loud explosions.

Janey and Joe and Rufus moved off. They didn't

want to look as though they were staring. If he'd ask them into his yard so they could really watch, they'd like that. Putt-putt! How hard he worked!

"I hope he fixes it soon," said Jane. Because she really did not care for all that noise.

But the mechanical genius never really got the motorcycle fixed. Every day Wallie Bangs would march home from school into his back yard, drop his trigonometry book on the ground and, sput-sput, soon he'd have the motor going. After a number of loud explosions the motor would run smoothly for a while. "There," people would say, "now he's going to turn her right side up and ride her away." But Wallie never did. He wasn't interested in riding. He was interested in fixing.

Occasionally the motorcycle was already right side up. Wallie Bangs would leap into the smooth, leather seat. "Hey, look!" someone would yell and everybody would stop what they were doing and watch.

"Isn't the fellow a wiz?" they'd all marvel. "He's going to ride that old thing away to Timbuctoo now."

But Wallie was not thinking of Timbuctoo or even Main Street. He was thinking about how the motor sounded. He'd suddenly pull valves,

push buttons, make the engine roar good and loud, and then bang! A few feeble clucks and the engine would die out.

"Sounds like a giant hen laying an egg," thought Jane.

On a quiet evening when people were sitting around reading the paper or were raking the leaves, suddenly, bang! the mechanical wizard had started fixing his motorcycle. He worked as late as he could see. He was very sorry when daylight saving time went out and he lost that extra hour. However he then worked far into the evening by the light of a shiny red flashlight. He had many flashlights of all sizes, and at night you could see him coming from a long way off, flashing one of his lights on and off.

Jane spent many moments watching Wallie at work in his back yard. She had never seen anyone work so hard.

"Don't you ever play?" she asked him once in a fit of courage.

Wallie Bangs did not answer. And Jane wondered how she had had the audacity to speak to such a mechanical wizard. To make up for it she wished she had something for him to fix. Skates, say. But she didn't have any skates.

Wallie certainly did like to take skates apart. Also dollar watches and clocks. Wires, screws, and tiny disks from these were strewn over his work table. He had Miss Buckle's washing machine apart too, and just the other day he had gotten hold of deaf Mr. Price's ear phones. He had plenty to keep him busy.

Jane's admiration for the mechanical genius grew. His absorbed air fascinated her. She felt it was too bad she did not have something he could fix. She watched Wallie come marching around the house with a handful of skates and she felt left out of things. She wished she had a pair of skates.

One day, as though in answer to her prayers, Mama called her into the house. Mama was counting yellow and orange coupons she had saved up from the wrappers of naphtha soap. They were stacked in neat piles of fifty on the kitchen table. Beside her was a little book with pictures of the things these coupons could be exchanged for.

"Janey," said Mama, "what shall we get with our coupons? We have a nice stack of them."

Jane thumbed through the book. There were cut-glass punch bowls with little cups hanging from hooks around the side. Miss Buckle had one of those. Also Mrs. Stokes. There were pots and pans, shiny aluminum ones. Did Mama want her to say, "How about this nice teakettle?" She skipped some pages and her eyes fell on a pair of skates.

Ball-bearin' skates!

She paused. That's what she'd like. But, of course, they should send for something for all the family. She looked at the skates again. She wished she had them for she was tired of borrowing one of Nancy's. She'd like to skate with two feet.

"I don't know," she said to Mama.

Mama was looking at her, smiling. "How about this pair of skates?" she asked.

So that's the way it was. Jane soon had a
bright shiny pair of ball-bearing skates and she
and Nancy had many good times with all four
feet on skates. They often skated on the white
sidewalk in front of Wallie Bangs' house.

Usually when Wallie Bangs marched around
the house he wouldn't even notice them.

Once in a while though he surprised them

with a remark like this: "Skates working all right?"

Or he'd look at them with an earnest frown and say: "Might need just a little tightening here and there to make them A number one."

Nancy said, "Don't let him have our skates. We'll never get them back."

But sometimes Jane felt that if Wallie Bangs fixed her skates they'd go faster than lightning.

One day when Nancy was home practicing her music, Jane glided out onto Wallie Bangs' sidewalk. Wallie Bangs came marching around from the back yard with a battery in his hand. He didn't look at Janey. But he did take a sidelong look at Janey's skates. Jane thought he looked at her skates the way a doctor looks at a patient, figuring out what's wrong. There was a thoughtful pucker on his brow, but he said nothing. He marched past her.

Jane thought she might have hurt his feelings since she had never asked him to fix her skates.

"Hey," she yelled before he reached the corner. "Would you like to fix my skates?"

"Thought those skates needed a bit o' fixin'," Wallie Bangs said, stopping short.

Jane took them off and she laid them at Wallie's feet. In no time at all Wallie was marching around to the back yard with her skates, just the way she had seen him dozens of times with all the others. But Jane followed him. She ran to catch up with him.

"Will you put my name on them like the shoemaker does when he's fixin' my shoes?" she asked, pursuing him into the cellar.

"A lot of nonsense," said Wallie, dropping them on his work bench.

"But my skates are bran' new and I wouldn't want you to get them mixed up with Clara Pringle's," Jane pleaded.

"Very well, then. What's your name?" asked Wallie, taking out a worn black notebook filled with smudges, numbers, and expert calculations.

Jane was startled. He didn't even know who she was yet and she lived right next door. But then, she quickly reasoned, how could you expect a mechanical wizard to keep track of the neighbors?

"I'm Jane, the middle Moffat," she said.

"No foolishness now," he said. But he wrote "J. the m.m." in his book. Then in just a few minutes he had Jane's skates all apart.

Jane backed up the stairs and out. "J. the m.m.," she muttered.

Later she said to Joe, "Gee, you should see the things he's got down there!"

"Yeh, I been down," said Joe, nodding his head appreciatively.

But Nancy was not impressed. She said, "Oh, Jane! Now when'll you ever get your skates back?"

"Oh, he'll fix mine soon," said Jane reassuringly. " 'Cause I live right next door."

But she watched Nancy skate off with a faint feeling of uneasiness. Her nice new ball-bearin' skates. When would she ever see them again?

She climbed onto the fence and she watched Wallie Bangs at work upon his motorcycle. Sput! Sput! He was as busy as ever on that. In spite of having a cellar full of skates, clocks, watches, and one ear phone to fix, he still spent practically every second fixing his motorcycle. Either he took things apart, or he fixed his motorcycle. Two things. Nothing else.

Jane watched him. Wallie Bangs, the mechanical wizard! Sput! Sput! She wished he'd fix her skates first though before he fixed that motorcycle. But goodness! What was she thinking? Fix little skates before a big motorcycle? Of course there wasn't any sense in that.

As days went on Jane missed her skates more and more. Nancy offered her one of hers now and again. But Janey refused. She was beginning to feel that she had made a mistake and that she should take the consequences.

One day Jane stood by the honeysuckle bush. Nancy had just skated out of the Moffats' front yard, backwards. Jane glided up and down the lawn a few times, pretending she too was on her skates again. Her ball-bearin' skates ... Just then Wallie Bangs came marching around the yard, a few skates dangling from his right hand. He went down in the cellar with them.

"Stay there and fix those skates," said Jane angrily. But she didn't say it out loud. After all he was the mechanical genius, and the whole school, in fact, the whole town, talked about him. Still when she saw him mount the cellar stairs and approach his motorcycle, drop his trigonometry book, thud! on the ground, her anger mounted again.

"Hey!" she said.

"Something need fixin'?" Wallie Bangs did not even look up. Just said, "Something need fixin'?" as he squatted down beside his motorcycle.

"My skates!" yelled Jane.

"Bring 'em over. Anything mechanical . . ."

"You got my skates! You've had 'em for two whole weeks! You could fix them!"

"On the contrary!"

"You could 'ave too!" yelled Jane. And then she ran, heart in throat.

She sat down on the green wicker rocker on the porch, behind the hop vines where Wallie Bangs could not see her. Here she was, a girl of ten, and she had yelled at the mechanical genius and asked when he was going to fix her skates. She wondered how she had dared. But it was easier the next day. And easier still the day after.

"Fix my skates," she'd yell the minute Wallie came marching around the house from school. And then she'd run. But Wallie acted as though he hadn't even heard. He'd press his chin deep down in his collar and study his motorcycle. In a little while Jane would screw up her courage again and dart back to the honeysuckle bush.

"Hey! Fix my skates!" she'd yell, and then scoot.

But Wallie looked neither to the left nor the right.

However, some of the other children in the neighborhood listened to Jane in amazement. What was this? Jane Moffat yelling at the mechanical wizard?

One day Clara Pringle wandered by, dragging Brud in his red tin express wagon. She heard Janey yell these words:

"Fix my skates, Wallie Bangs, if you're such a mechanical genius!"

And then Janey ran.

Clara Pringle watched. Nothing happened. The mechanical genius just kept on working as though nothing had been said. So Clara turned around and pulled Brud into Wallie Bangs' back yard. Pausing a good ten steps away from the mechanical genius, she said:

"Are my skates ready yet?"

Wallie Bangs replied with a long scientific discourse

which left Clara blinking. And, of course, still without her skates. But she hastily pushed Brud out of Wallie's back yard, when he said:

"What about that old wagon of yours? Goin' smoothly?"

"Run, Clara, run!" shouted Jane, who was watching proceedings from behind the honeysuckle bush.

And Clara escaped with Brud's express wagon.

Others came now to Wallie Bangs and asked for their skates. Some did as Janey did, shouted from a distance, "Hey, fix my skates!" And some were more polite. They went up to Wallie Bangs, frequently proffering him a stick of candy. He seemed to like "crispy crunches" the best, although he ate jelly beans or anything else with the same preoccupied mien.

"Wallie," they said, "would you mind putting my skates together? They may not have been perfect before but at least I could skate on them. What good are they to me now, all apart and down in your cellar?"

But usually Wallie just shrugged his shoulders, pulled his gray sweater up in back so he wouldn't stretch it, and squatted down beside his motorcycle. Sput! Sput! He'd make the engine roar so loud everybody would jump out of

the way, expecting it to go all by itself. Or he'd say, "Run along, children. Very busy now. As soon as possible I'll get at those skates!"

He'd say "skates" rather disdainfully, making the boy or girl feel like two cents for interrupting.

After a while the little girls grew tired of getting lectures on thermodynamics when all they wanted was their skates. The same with little boys and their dollar watches. More and more of them, like Jane, began to taunt Wallie Bangs every time they saw him, with a shout:

"Hey, fix my skates!"

These were not the boys and girls who proffered him candy. These were the boys and girls who often gathered on Janey's back fence. They sat there and they watched Wallie Bangs at work.

"There he is!"

"Mechanical genius! Pooh!"

"Why doesn't he get anything fixed then?"

They sat there on the fence and they grew angry. This was perfect skating weather. And where were their skates? Down in Wallie Bangs' cellar, all apart.

They wondered what they could do. Wallie Bangs paid absolutely no attention to their taunts, their jibes, or their skates. What could they do?

"I know what," said Jane. "I'm just going over there and get my skates, broke or not."

Dead silence greeted this.

Of course that's what they would all like to do, just march over there and get their skates and their watches. But ... well, next to the oldest inhabitant, Wallie Bangs was probably the most important person in Cranbury. Who would have the nerve to march over there

and into his back yard and take his skates?
Jane did.

She lowered herself off the high board fence.
Not into Wallie's yard. Into her own yard. For
she was going to attack from the front. The children watched her disappear around the Moffats'
little house in silence. They watched through the
grape vines for her to appear in Wallie Bangs'
back yard.

"There she is!" cried Nancy Stokes excitedly.

Yes! There she was! Jane was marching around
Wallie Bangs' house. She did feel scared. But
after all they were her skates. Supposing Mama
was fixing a dress for Miss Buckle, and Mama
took the dress all apart and just wouldn't put it
together again. Of course Miss Buckle could come
and take her pieces of dress back home with her
any time she wanted to. Take shoes too. If the
shoemaker kept Janey's shoes there in the shoe
shop without fixing them, she could go in and
get them. They were her shoes. And these were
her skates. All the same she did feel scared inside. After all, this wasn't Mama or the shoemaker. This was the mechanical wizard!

She marched into Wallie Bangs' yard now.
She saw the children on the fence bent over and
watching her through the grape vines. She waved

to them but only out of braggadocio, for she really was scared. Thank goodness the cellar doors were open. Of course Wallie kept them open so he could get in and out quickly with his batteries and his pieces of wire and springs.

Right now Wallie didn't seem to see Jane at all. He kept pulling plugs and valves and making the engine roar. All the same, just as she was about to step down the cellar steps, he said:

"Anything mechanical . . . just bring 'em over . . ."

"I'm goin' to get my skates," cried Jane, and she darted down the cellar.

But goodness! How was she ever going to find hers among all these dismantled parts? She looked about in despair. Her nice new ball-bearin' skates! Where were they? One pile under the set tub looked new and shiny. Maybe these were hers. She picked up one of the wheels and a grimy piece of paper fluttered out. "J. the m.m." it said. Hurrah! These were her skates. She gathered them up and ran out.

"No foolishness now," said Wallie Bangs without looking to the left or the right.

Jane ran home while the children on the back fence cheered.

"Come on," they yelled. "Let's get our skates! Janey got hers!"

"It's easy," said Jane. "I'll show you. Just follow me."

They all marched into Wallie Bangs' back yard. They approached cautiously, retreating to the fence whenever Wallie shifted his position, but then advancing again when he settled back to work. He really did not appear to be aware of their presence. Once, however, when they were right up to the cellar stairs, Wallie Bangs dropped his battery and came marching over in their direction. They fled to the honeysuckle bush, ready to dart through it if necessary. But Wallie was paying no attention to them. All he wanted apparently was a little piece of wire from the cellar.

"Anything mechanical . . . just bring 'em over," he said, bending over his motorcycle again. The children all came back. This time they rushed into the cellar. Soon they were all running out with armfuls of wheels, straps, and other skate parts.

"Wallie Bangs, we got our skates," they yelled.

Wallie did not answer. Putt! Putt! He made his engine roar. After all, thought Jane, he might be right in the middle of fixing his motorcycle

once and for all at this very minute. Why should he pay attention to skate parts?

Clara Pringle ran down to Pleasant Street spreading the news.

"Come on," she yelled. "Everybody get their skates!"

And children began gathering from Pleasant Street, Elm Street, and even Second Avenue, because good news of this sort quickly spread. They crawled through the honeysuckle bush from the Moffats' yard and ducked into Wallie Bangs' cellar like rabbits going down a rabbit hole. Then, blinking, out they came with skates, watches, and clocks. They quickly made their get-away for no one knew how Wallie Bangs was going to take this insurrection.

The way he took it was just to make his engine roar.

When finally all the children had left, Joey helped Jane fit her skates together. She certainly was glad she had made Wallie write "J. the m.m." on hers. Some boys and girls had had to be content with just one or two wheels. All of a sudden Wallie appeared on his side of the honeysuckle bush.

"Skates need a little fixin'?" he asked.

Jane and Joey hast-
ily retreated to their little square porch.

"No, thanks," said
Jane politely. After all
he still was the mechan-
ical genius even after
the events of the day.

Wallie Bangs never did get around to putting
Miss Buckle's washing machine together and after a few weeks of sending her laundry to the
family wet wash she called in the handy man,
and soon things were running smoothly in her
household again.

As for Mr. Price's ear phones, he said, "Oh, let
'em go. I'll be glad to wait until the boy fixes his
motorcycle. Ear phones can wait."

"You're lucky," said Mrs. Price, stuffing her
ears with cotton after a particularly loud bang
from Wallie's back yard.

Sometimes Jane wondered if Wallie's feelings
had been hurt by everybody going and getting
their skates. She finally decided that this was
not so. His mind was on his motorcycle. He had
no time for skates. And he always asked her,
when she was skating on his white sidewalk,
just as though nothing had ever happened:

"Skates need a little fixin'? Just bring 'em over
. . . anything mechanical . . ."

6

A LETTER FROM SANTA CLAUS

Rufus wanted a pony. In this he was no different from every other small boy. Every Christmas Rufus asked Santa Claus for one. In his letters to Santa Claus, a pony always topped the list. Oh, of course, he used to ask for other things too, a bicycle, a top, an engine, toy soldiers, a jack-knife, but the pony was what he wanted more than anything else in the world. He tried in his letters to point this out to Santa Claus. For instance, in one letter he put a gold star by the word "pony." In another he wrote "pony" in red crayon. Still Santa Claus didn't seem to catch on, and he never brought a pony. He brought other fine things, pea blowers, horns, drums, and Rufus was grateful for them but they didn't answer that longing he had inside for a pony.

How did he get it into his head he wanted a pony? Well, one day a couple of years ago, when the Moffats were living in the yellow house on New Dollar Street, a man had come along leading a black and white pony. You could have your picture taken sitting on its back for ten cents. Mama said Rufus should have one taken. She would frame it and put it on the mantel. So the man picked Rufus up and set him on the pony's back and took his picture. Then the man let Rufus ride the pony as far as Hughie Pudge's house. There, however, he had to get down and let Hughie Pudge get up, for he was going to have his picture taken too. Ever since that time when he had felt real pony flesh between his legs, Rufus had wanted a pony just terribly.

Last Christmas Santa Claus had brought him a brown felt pony on wheels, all right for very small children perhaps, but certainly not the thing for him. After this experience Rufus decided he'd better add the word "ALIVE" after "pony."

This Christmas Mama said to the children, "Do not ask Santa Claus for too much this year because, you know, there is a terrible war going on in Europe and Santa Claus will need an extra

large amount of things for the Belgian children."
So one evening, after the supper dishes had been
cleared away, Jane and Rufus took pencil and
paper to the kitchen table, pushed back the red-
checked tablecloth and wrote their letters to
Santa Claus.

Jane wrote:

> *Dear Santy Claus,*
> *Please bring me*
> *Two-storied pencil box*
> *Flexible flier sled*
> *Box of paints*
> *Princess and Curdie.*

Then she stopped for a moment. She would like
to say, "Please don't bring any material for a
dress or anything to wear, or for practical's sake."
But perhaps Santa Claus would not think that
was polite, so she signed,

> *With love,*
> *Jane Moffat.*

She looked over at Rufus' letter. "Have you
finished?" she asked.

"Not quite," he answered. His tongue was between his teeth and he was working very hard.

Jane watched him curiously for he was no longer writing but was drawing something on his letter with brown crayon.

"How many things you ask for?" he demanded presently.

"Four," said Jane.

"Four!" repeated Rufus. "I only ast for one," he announced with satisfaction.

When he finally laid down his crayon, he held his letter up and surveyed it approvingly.

"Can I look at it?" asked Jane.

Looking at one another's letters to Santa Claus was usually an unheard-of procedure. They were for Santa's eyes alone. But this letter Rufus was proud of and he pushed it over to Jane with a magnanimous gesture.

This was Rufus' letter:

"Gee, that's nice," approved Jane.

"Think he'll know what I mean?"

"Sure."

"Maybe I better add the words 'real one' under the picture just to make sure," said Rufus.

So he carefully printed the words "REAL ONE" under his drawing and was convinced that now he had made it plain to Santa Claus what he wanted for Christmas. He and Jane took their letters to the kitchen stove, lifted the lid, and dropped them into the red hot coals. The draught whisked them up the chimney and the charred letters were gone.

"Funny he can read them when they are burned up like that," said Rufus.

"He just can," said Jane with finality.

Rufus went back to the kitchen table and wrote another letter with a picture of an "ALIVE" pony on it. This he gave to Mama to put in her bag and mail in the big Post Office tomorrow when she went to town.

"I'm sure he'll get one or the other of them," said Rufus.

Jane sat down before the kitchen fire to warm her toes.

"Dear God," she prayed, "tell Santy Claus to bring him the pony."

She could not bear to think of another Christmas Day with no pony for Rufus. Then she began thinking about what to give Mama this Christmas. Something especially lovely. What was the loveliest thing she could think of? She watched the sparkling coals and suddenly she had a wonderful idea. The gift should be a beautiful bag, brocaded and sparkling with gold and silver threads, all embroidered together into a gorgeous pattern. Yes! She had seen such a bag once in a store window on Chapel Street in town. Certainly that was the gift for Mama.

She called Joe and Rufus. She didn't call Sylvie

because Sylvie already had all her presents wrapped and hidden on the top shelf of the pantry.

"How much money you got?" she asked them.

"What do you want to know for?" they both countered.

Jane told them about the bag. She painted it in glowing colors. "It'll be lovely. It'll be shiny all over," she ended up. Rufus and Joe were impressed. They liked the idea. Well now! A brocaded bag for Mama. That was something!

"Well, how much money have you got?" asked Jane impatiently. "Because I don't have enough just by myself. And this brockated bag'll be from the whole three of us."

Rufus disappeared in the closet under the stairs and came back with his old Prince Albert tobacco box he kept his treasures in. Among the bottle tops in it he found a few pennies, six in all. He dropped them in Jane's lap.

Joe put his hand in his pocket. He kept his money there, when he had any, like a grown man. He pulled out two nickels and two pennies and dropped them in Jane's lap. Jane opened the little Chinese purse that Mama and Sylvie had brought her from New York's Chinatown. A nickel and four pennies fell out of this. Altogether

it looked quite a pile. She scooped it up in the palm of her hand.

"Twenty-seven cents," she announced with satisfaction, shaking the coins up and down, up and down.

"Will that buy one of those bags?" asked Joe incredulously.

"Oh, no," replied Jane scornfully. "They cost a dollar at least. I'm goin' to make this brockated bag."

"Supposin' you don't finish it before Christmas?" asked Joe. "Then I'll have nothin' for Mama."

"I'll finish it," said Jane positively. Again she painted the bag she would make in glowing terms, for she saw that their enthusiasm was lagging. She rolled the words lovingly on her tongue, gold threads, silver threads, cerise, peacock blue, threads of silk and satin . . . brocaded . . . Well, they were won over again.

"Tomorrow we'll go to Aberdeen's and get the things," she concluded, exhausted from all this persuading, and putting all the coins in her purse.

The next day it was snowing very hard. It had begun in the middle of the night. Silently a soft, thick mantle had been laid over the earth and it was growing thicker by the minute. Jane and

Joe and Rufus ran to the front window and looked out. Marvelous! The first deep snow of winter! They waved good-by to Sylvie who was making her way with difficulty through the deep drifts.

"Where's she goin'?" asked Rufus.

"To the Parish House to rehearse for the Christmas tableau," said Jane. "Come on. Get ready to go to Aberdeen's and get the things."

"All right, let's go," said Rufus impatiently.

They put on their rubbers. "Mine leak," said Jane, looking at the holes in the heels and toes. "But never mind, Santy Claus," she breathed, "I don't care a thing about whole rubbers." Rubbers would be worse to see on Christmas morning than material for a dress, she was thinking.

"Where are you going?" asked Mama.

Jane made grimaces at Rufus and Joe to keep them from saying, "Aberdeen's." This was to be a real surprise.

"We're just going out to play in the snow," said Jane carelessly.

"All right," said Mama, "but don't be gallivanting all over town. And come in when your feet get wet."

"All right. Good-by, Mama." And they each ran in to kiss her good-by, giving her a good hug besides. "Wait till she sees the brockated bag she's going to get," they thought.

Out into the snow they ran. The whole world was white. Soon they looked like snow men.

"Boy, oh, boy, I'll have plenty of shoveling to do when we get back," said Joe.

Although they could walk on the sidewalk, most of which had been cleared by the snow plow, they preferred to walk through the deep snow on the side of the pavements. They sank into the soft snow as far as their knees. This was good fun. After a while Jane said, "We better hurry. And anyway, my chilblains are itching me. And I want to get home and start that bag."

At last they reached Aberdeen's department store, the only large store in Cranbury. Rufus

ran up to the show window and stretched his arms out wide. "Up to here is mine," he said, almost losing his balance. "And up to here is mine," laughed Jane, stretching her arms so wide she felt as though she would burst. It was still snowing so hard they could hardly see through the window. They did see that there was nothing there as pretty as the bag that Jane was going to make for Mama.

They pushed open the door. They sniffed the strange smells here, bolts of new material, rubber raincoats and overshoes, powder and perfumes. Because it was such a bad day, there were few people shopping. Joe, Jane, and Rufus stood at the goods counter and waited. Mrs. Aberdeen herself, dressed in many sweaters and a black apron, came to wait on them. She had a pencil stuck in the bun of her hair, a tape measure around her neck, and a pair of scissors strung on a black silk ribbon dangling from her bosom. Mrs. Aberdeen looked more like Madame-the-bust than anyone else in Cranbury.

"What do you want, children?" she asked briskly.

Jane looked at her, wondering how to begin. It was clear that Mrs. Aberdeen was not going to guess "brockated bag" just by looking at the three Moffats.

"Well, speak up," she said, more briskly still. "A spool of thread? A yard of elastic? Garters? Buttons?"

"No," said Jane. "We, that is, I, that is, we're all giving it, but I am making it, want to make a bag for Mama for Christmas."

"Oh, well ... I see ... well, now, how much money can you spend?"

Jane opened the little Chinese purse and the nickels and pennies rolled out on the counter.

"Twenty-seven cents," said Jane. "And I want to 'broider the bag."

"Yes. Well, twenty-seven cents won't buy much."

"A brockated bag," Jane breathed, but Mrs. Aberdeen didn't hear her.

"Here's a nice piece of goods you can have for that money," said Mrs. Aberdeen, holding up a piece of blue calico.

"I want to 'broider the bag," Jane repeated faintly.

Mrs. Aberdeen pulled out a skein of white embroidery cotton. "There," she said kindly. "I'm sure that will make a very nice bag."

"These things don't shine. Something is wrong," thought Jane, almost sobbing. But she paid the money and Mrs. Aberdeen deftly wrapped up the cloth and the embroidery thread in crackling green paper. With a real, bought package under her arm, Jane felt better. Then, too, the plain blue calico was out of sight and her vision of the brocaded bag returned in full force. It danced before her, a lovely elusive thing that quickened her pace. Joe and Rufus practically had to run to keep up with her.

"Will *that* be the brockated bag?" panted Joe.

"Wait and see," replied Jane with such an air of confidence that any doubts that Joe and Rufus might have had were cast immediately to the winds. By the time they reached home, the brocaded bag was again the beautiful teasing vision they all had had.

Mama was in the kitchen so they unwrapped the green package in the little green and white parlor with eager fingers. They would not have been surprised had the blue calico changed into a brocaded bag on the way home. However, the blue calico was still blue calico, though it was obvious from Jane's joyful spirits that she would have this transformed into the other lovely thing in no time.

During the next few days, Jane worked hard on the bag. She cut it out and sewed it up, every stitch by hand. She embroidered "MAMA" on one side of it with the white embroidery thread. On the other, she embroidered a daisy. When she finished it, she held it up and surveyed it with satisfaction. The brocaded bag! She saw it flash and sparkle and gleam with different shining colors. It was the very bag she had seen in the big store window in town.

In excitement she called Joe and Rufus in to see the finished bag. She dangled it before them, walked mincingly with it on her arm as elegant ladies do, thinking perhaps she looked like Mrs. Stokes.

"Is *that* a brockated bag?" they asked wonderingly.

"Yes!" said Jane. "Isn't it lovely?" And she walked up to the mirror to look at herself with the pretty thing. Her eyes fell on the bag. What they saw there was a very plain blue calico bag with a crooked "MAMA" embroidered on one

side and a humped-back daisy on the other. She looked down at the real bag hanging on her arm. The fair vision of the brocaded bag vanished completely and forever. She fell silent. The boys said nothing. After all, they had never seen a brocaded bag. In a while Jane said thoughtfully, "It will be good to keep buttons in."

They wrapped it up and made a card for it, "To Mama, with love from Joe, Rufus and Jane," and hid it where Mama would not be able to find it.

At last it was Christmas Eve. The four Moffats were making decorations for the tree, angels of gold and silver paper, baskets for candy and cookies, chains of colored paper, cornucopias for popcorn. The kitchen table was quite covered with scraps of paper and sticky with flour-and-water paste which Rufus had dabbed around by mistake. Sylvie had shown him how to make the chains of circles of bright paper. It was true that all of his chains were not linked together properly. His chain broke into short separate links that hung aimlessly from the whole. However, Sylvie said this did not matter in the slightest. Sylvie and Mama were going to help Santa Claus out by having the tree trimmed before he came late tonight. At present they were busy making the spiced Santa Claus cookies for the tree. How good they did smell!

"It is time now to hang your stockings," said Mama.

The four of them, even Sylvie, tore off to their rooms to find stockings that didn't have any holes in them so none of the good things would fall out of the heel or toe. They tacked these onto the wainscoting behind the kitchen stove, right handy for Santa Claus.

Now there was really nothing to do but go to bed. Rufus and Janey went first. They stripped off their clothes before the kitchen fire. They put on their outing flannel bed-socks and nightclothes and raced noisily up the stairs to bed.

But not to sleep! Not yet! They talked and laughed, smothering their giggles under the bed-clothes. They whispered, "What do you think Santy Claus will bring us?"

"Let's stay awake all night and watch for Santy Claus," said Rufus.

"What are Mama and Sylvie so mysterious about?" Jane asked.

"What do you think Santy will bring?" Rufus asked this for the hundredth time, although there was really little doubt in his mind. Had he not written Santa Claus the same letter every night

for a week, telling him to bring a real live pony,
even showing by drawings exactly what he
meant? Goodness knows how many of these letters had found their way to Santa Claus. So
many probably that Rufus had grown rather
worried at the last and varied his letter to read,

> DEAR SANTY,
>   Please bring me a live pony. ONE
> is plenty.
>   RUFUS

"Goodness," he chuckled, "if Santy brought a
pony for every letter I wrote! ... But I guess
he'll know better than that."

In spite of themselves, they began to grow
sleepy. Then Joe came to bed and talked for a
while, but soon Joey and Rufus became quiet
and Jane knew they were asleep. Jane stayed
awake, however. Her chilblains itched her. But
she wasn't thinking about them so much. She
was thinking about Rufus and that pony he
expected.

"He certainly does want that pony," she thought.
"He wants that pony harder than I have ever
wanted anything."

And this year he was so positive that Santa

would bring one. Nevertheless, Jane had a sinking feeling in her stomach that Christmas morning would come and there just would not be a pony for Rufus. What should she do? His disappointment would be more than she could bear. "Something oughter be done," she worried, "but what?"

Just then Sylvie came upstairs and climbed into bed.

"Asleep, Janekin?" she asked softly.

Jane didn't answer, pretending to be asleep. There was no use troubling Sylvie about this pony business too. After a while she could tell from Sylvie's breathing that she was asleep. For a long time Jane lay there. Supposing she stayed awake this year and listened for Santa Claus? A word in his ear about the pony might work wonders. Other years she had meant to do this, but somehow morning had always come and the stockings had been filled as by magic and she would realize that she had gone to sleep and missed Santa Claus after all. He had come in the middle of the night. This year would be different though. She would stay awake—yes, she would.

She listened to all the night noises: the frost making the windowpanes creak; Mama calling Catherine-the-cat; Mama turning the key in the latch, winding the clock, shaking down the kitchen fire and the fire in the parlor. Finally she heard Mama drop first one shoe and then the other with a soft thud to the floor, and she knew that Mama too was in bed.

Now all she had to do was to listen for Santa Claus. Surely he would be here soon. It must be very late—midnight, probably. She would stay awake and stay awake . . . She would say to him, "Please, Santy, a pony for Rufus . . ." The first thing she would hear would be the sleighbells and the reindeer's hooves on the roof . . . She must stay awake and . . .

In telling Nancy about this night later, Jane was positive she had stayed awake. Positive that just as the clock in the sitting room downstairs struck twelve, Santa Claus had stood beside her bed and gently turned her over. His frosty beard had even brushed her cheek. And he had whispered something in her ear. But just as she was about to speak to him, he had vanished and the sleighbells tinkled off in the distance.

She sat up in bed. Sylvie was sleeping peacefully. Santa Claus had gone. Of that she was sure. Oh, why had he not waited for her to speak? Softly she crept out of bed, felt her way past the chiffonier into the hall, and stole down the creak-ing stairs to the kitchen. She was grateful for the faint light that shone from the kitchen stove. Finding the matches, she struck one. Catherine-the-cat's eyes shone green and examined her with keen disapproval. Paying no attention to her, Jane glanced swiftly behind the stove. There the four stockings hung, bulging now. Yes, that proved it. Santa had been here just now and had come to her side to give her some message.

She glanced around the room and peeked into the little parlor where the Christmas tree was shining. There was no pony about. That was certain. She tiptoed to the back window and

pressed her face against the pane. The moon shone over the white snow, making a light almost as bright as day. If there had been a pony out there, she would know it. There just wasn't any pony and there was no use hoping for it any longer. That was why Santa had come to her bedside. He knew she was awake and waiting and he had a good reason for not bringing the pony, and that's what he had wanted to tell her. What was the reason? She thought for a moment. Then she knew. She lighted another match, found a piece of brown wrapping paper and a pencil. Crouching on the floor near the stove she wrote,

> *Dear Rufus,*
> *All the ponies are at the war.*
> *Your friend,*
> *Santy Claus.*

She tucked this note in the top of Rufus' stocking and went back to bed. Shivering, she pressed her cold self against Sylvie and fell sound asleep.

The next thing she knew, Sylvie was shaking her and shaking her and screaming, "Merry Christmas, Merry Christmas!" Jane jumped out of bed, pulled a blanket around her, danced wildly out of the room screaming, "Merry Christmas, Merry Christmas!" Mama gave them each a sweet hug and a kiss and said, "Merry Christmas, every-body." The whole house echoed and Catherine-the-cat chased her tail for the first time in five and a half years.

They grabbed their stockings and raced back to bed with them, for the house was still bitterly cold. A sudden yell from Rufus interrupted everything.

"Whoops!" he shouted. "Whoops! Listen to this! Ma! ma! Listen! I've had a letter from Santy Claus."

Rufus jumped out of bed and tore through the house like a cyclone, the others following him.

"Listen to this," he said again, when they were finally collected before the kitchen fire. " 'Dear Rufus,' it says. 'Dear Rufus, All the ponies are at the war,' and it's signed 'Your friend, Santy Claus!' Imagine a letter from Santy Claus himself!"

Mama put on her glasses and examined the note carefully.

"H-m-m-m," she said.

"Gee," said Rufus, "wait till I show this to Eddie Bangs. He's always boastin' of his auto-graps collection. He's got President Taft, Mayor Harley, Chief Mulligan. But he ain't got Santy Claus."

Jane could see that having a letter from Santa

Claus himself softened considerably Rufus' disappointment in not getting a real live pony.

When calm was somewhat restored, the gifts were taken from the tree. These were some of the most exciting moments: When Mama opened her "brockated bag" and said, "This will be elegant to keep buttons in"; when Rufus opened his toy village—houses, trees, grocery boys on bicycles, delivery men with horses and wagons, firemen and fire engines, a postman, a policeman and a milkman—yes, a complete village to lay out with streets and parks; when Jane opened her miniature grocery store, with tiny boxes of real cocoa and salt, sacks of sugar and the smallest jars of real honey; when Sylvie opened a huge box and drew out a fluffy white dress Mama had secretly made for her first ball, the Junior-Senior promenade; and when Joe opened a long, slim package that had a shining clarinet in it! "Boy, oh, boy," was all he could say.

But now it was time for Sylvie to go to church to take her part in the Christmas tableau. Of course all the Moffats were going to watch her and join in the beautiful Christmas carols. Before they left, however, Mama gathered them all around the tree and they sang:

> "Hark! The herald angels sing
> Glory to the newborn King.
> Peace on earth and mercy mild
> God and sinners reconciled!"

7

THE MIDDLE BEAR

When a play was given at the town hall, Sylvie was usually the only one of the four Moffats who was in it. However, once in a while the others were in a play. For instance, Rufus had been the smallest of the seven dwarfs. And once Janey had been a butterfly. She had not been an altogether successful butterfly, though, for she had tripped on the sole of her stocking, turning a

somersault all across the stage. And whereas
Joey was rarely in a play, he was often in charge
of switching the lights on and off.

Jane liked the plays at the Town Hall. In fact
she liked them better than the moving pictures.
In the moving pictures Jane always found it
difficult to tell the good man from the bad man.
Especially if they both wore black mustaches. Of
course the pianist usually played ominous music
just before the bad man came on the scene, and
that helped. Even so, Jane preferred the plays at
the Town Hall. There she had no trouble at all
telling the good from the bad.

Now there was to be a play at the Town Hall,
"The Three Bears," and all four of the Moffats
were going to be in it. Miss Chichester, the dancing school teacher, was putting it on. But the
money for the tickets was not going into her
pocket or into the Moffats' pocket, even though
they were all in the play. The money was to help
pay for the new parish house. The old one had
burned down last May and now a new one was
being built. "The Three Bears" was to help raise
the money to finish it. A benefit performance, it
was called.

In this benefit performance, Sylvie was to play
the part of Goldilocks. Joey was to be the big

bear, Rufus the little bear, and Janey the middle bear. Jane had not asked to be the middle bear. It just naturally came out that way. The middle Moffat was going to be the middle bear.

As a rule Joey did not enjoy the idea of acting in a play any more than he liked going to dancing school. However, he felt this play would be different. He felt it would be like having a disguise on, to be inside of a bear costume. And Jane felt the same way. She thought the people in the audience would not recognize her as the butterfly who turned a somersault across the stage, because she would be comfortably hidden inside her brown bear costume. As for Rufus, he hoped that Sylvie, the Goldilocks of this game, would not sit down too hard on that nice little chair of his and really break it to bits. It was such a good chair, and he wished he had it at home.

Mama was making all the costumes, even the bear heads. A big one for Joey, a little one for

Rufus, and a middle-sized one for Jane. Of course she wasn't making them out of bear fur; she was using brown outing flannel.

Now Jane was trying on her middle bear costume. She stepped into the body of the costume and then Mama put the head on her.

"Make the holes for the eyes big enough," Jane begged. "So I'll see where I'm going and won't turn somersaults."

"Well," said Mama, "if I cut the eyes any larger you will look like a deep sea diver instead of a bear."

"Oh, well . . ." said Jane hastily. "A bear's got to look like a bear. Never mind making them any bigger, then."

Besides being in the play, each of the Moffats also had ten tickets to sell. And since Rufus really was too little to go from house to house and street to street selling tickets, the other three Moffats had even more to dispose of. Forty tickets!

At first Jane wondered if a girl should sell tickets to a play she was going to be in. Was that being conceited? Well, since the money was for the new parish house and not for the Moffats, she finally decided it was all right to sell the tickets. Besides, she thought, who would recognize her as the girl who sold tickets once she was inside her bear costume?

Sylvie sold most of her tickets like lightning to the ladies in the choir. But Joey's and Janey's tickets became grimier and grimier, they had such trouble disposing of them. Nancy Stokes said she would help even though she went to a different parish house. She and Joey and Jane went quietly and politely up on people's verandas and rang the bell.

"Buy a ticket for the benefit of the new parish house?" was all they meant to say. But very often no one at all answered the bell.

"They can't all be away," said Nancy. "Do you think they hide behind the curtains when they see us coming?"

"Oh, no," said Jane. "You see it'd be different if the money was for us. But it isn't. It's a benefit. Why should they hide?"

One lady said she was very sorry but she was making mincemeat. "See?" she said, holding up her hands. They were all covered with mincemeat. So she could not buy a ticket. Not possibly, and she closed the door in their faces.

"She could wash her hands," said Nancy angrily. The children called this lady "mincemeat," ever after. Of course she never knew it.

Yes, the tickets were very hard to sell. But little by little the pile did dwindle. If only everybody were like Mrs. Stokes, they would go very fast. She bought four tickets! Jane was embarrassed.

"Tell your mother she doesn't have to buy all those tickets just 'cause all of us are in the play," she instructed Nancy.

But all the Stokes insisted they really wanted to go. And even if none of the Moffats were in it, they would still want to go, for the play would help to build a new parish house. What nice people! thought Jane. Here they were, a family who went to the white church, buying tickets to help build a parish house for Janey's church. She hoped she would be a good middle bear, so they would be proud they knew her.

At last it was the night of the play. The four Moffats knew their lines perfectly. This was not surprising, considering they all lived in the same house and could practice their lines any time they wanted to. And, besides this, they had had two rehearsals, one in regular clothes and one in their bear costumes.

When Jane reached the Town Hall, she was surprised to find there were many features on the program besides "The Three Bears." The

Gillespie twins were going to give a piano duet. "By the Brook," it was called. A boy was going to play the violin. Someone else was going to toe dance. And Miss Beale was going to sing a song. A big program. And the Moffats, all of them except Mama, were going to watch this whole performance from behind the scenes. They could not sit in the audience with the regular people with their bear costumes on, for that would give the whole show away.

Jane fastened her eye to a hole in the curtain. Mama had not yet come. Of course Mama would have to sit out front there with the regular people, even though she had made the costumes. The only people who had arrived so far were Clara Pringle and Brud. They were sitting in the front row and Jane wondered how they had gotten in because the front door that all the regular people were supposed to use wasn't even open yet.

When Jane wasn't peering through a hole in the curtain, Joey or Rufus was. Each one hoped he would be the first to see Mama when she came in. Or now and then they tried to squeeze through the opening at the side of the asbestos curtain. But the gnarled little janitor shook his head at them. So they stayed inside.

Sylvie was busy putting make-up on herself and on the dancers' faces. Jane watched them enviously. The only trouble with wearing a bear costume, she thought, was that she couldn't have her face painted. Well, she quickly consoled herself, she certainly would not have stage fright inside her bear head. Whereas she might if there were just paint on her face. "Somebody has been sitting in my chair," she rehearsed her lines. She stepped into her bear costume. But before putting on her head, she helped Rufus into his bear uniform. He didn't call it a costume. A uniform. A bear uniform. Jane set his head on his shoulders, found his two eyes for him so he could see out, and the little bear was ready.

Joey had no difficulty stepping into his costume and even in finding his own two eyes. Now the big bear and the little bear were ready. Jane looked around for her head, to put it on. Where was it?

"Where's my head?" she asked. "My bear head."

Nobody paid any attention to her. Miss Chichester was running back and forth and all around, giving an order here and an order there. Once as she rushed by, causing a great breeze, Jane yelled to make herself heard, "How can we act 'The Three Bears' unless I find my middle bear head?"

"Not just now. I'm too busy," was all Miss Chichester said.

Everybody was too busy to help Jane find her head. Sylvie was helping the toe dancer dress. Joey was busy running around doing this and doing that for Miss Chichester. And the little old janitor was busy tightening ropes and making sure the lights were working. Rufus could not be torn from a hole in the curtain. He was looking for Mama.

Jane sighed. Everybody's busy, she thought. She rummaged around in a big box of costumes. Maybe her bear head had been stuck in it. She

found a dragon head and tried it on. How would that be? She looked in the mirror. The effect was interesting. But, no, she could not wear this, for a bear cannot be a dragon.

Goodness, thought Jane. The curtain will go up, and the middle bear won't be a whole bear. This was worse than tripping over her stocking the time she was a butterfly. Maybe Joey and Rufus somehow or another had two heads on. They didn't, though, just their own. Phew, it was warm inside these bear costumes. Jane stood beside Rufus and looked through another small hole in the curtain. Oh! The big door was open! People were beginning to arrive. And what kind of a bear would she be without a head? Maybe she wouldn't be allowed to be a bear at all. But there certainly could not be three bears without a middle one.

"Don't worry," said Rufus, not moving an inch from his spot. "Lend you mine for half the play . . ."

"Thanks," said Jane. "But we all have to have our heads on all through the whole thing."

The Stokes were coming in! Jane felt worried. The only person who might be able to fix a new bear head for her in a hurry was Mama. Oh, if she had only made a couple of spare heads. But

Mama wasn't coming yet. Jane resolved to go and meet her. She put on her tam and her chinchilla coat over her bear costume. Then she ran down the three narrow steps into the Hall. She crouched low in her coat in order not to give away the fact that she was clad in a bear costume. Nobody on this side of the curtain was supposed to know what people on her side of the curtain had on until the curtain rolled up. Surprise. That's what was important in a play.

Mr. Buckle was coming in now, walking towards the front row. Jane stooped low, with her knees bent beneath her. In front her coat nearly reached the ground. From the way she looked from the front, few would guess that she was the middle bear. Of course her feet showed. They were encased in the brown costume. But she might be a brownie or even a squirrel.

"Hello, Mr. Buckle," said Jane. "I'm in a hurry . . ."

"Where are you going, middle Moffat?" he asked. "Aren't you the prima donna?"

"No. Just the middle bear."

"Well, that's fine. The middle Moffat is the middle bear."

"Yes. Or I was until I lost my head."

"Oh, my," said Mr. Buckle. "This then is

not your head?" he asked, pointing to her tam.

"Yes, but not my bear head. I don't mean bare head. Bear head! B-e-a-r. That kind of head."

"Mystifying. Very mystifying," said Mr. Buckle, settling himself slowly in a seat in the front row.

"You'll see later," said Jane, running down the aisle.

She ran all the way home. But the house was dark. Mama had already left. And she must have gone around the other way or Jane would have passed her. Jane raced back to the Town Hall. There! Now! The lights were dim. The entertainment had begun. Jane tried to open the side door. Chief Mulligan was guarding this entrance. He did not want to let her in at first. He thought she was just a person. But when she showed him her costume, he opened the door just wide enough for her. The bear costume was as good as a password.

The toe dancer was doing the split. Jane tiptoed up the three steps and went backstage, wondering what would happen now. The show always goes on. There was some comfort in that thought. Somehow, someone would fix her head. Or possibly while she was gone her middle bear head had been found. She hoped she would not have to act with her head bare.

Miss Chichester snatched her.

"Oh, there you are, Jane! Hop into your costume, dear."

"I'm in it," said Jane. "But I can't find my middle bear head."

"Heavens!" said Miss Chichester, grasping her own head. "What else will go wrong?"

Jane looked at her in surprise. What else *had* gone wrong? Had others lost worse than their heads?

"Where's the janitor?" Miss Chichester asked. "Maybe he let his grandchildren borrow it."

Jane knew he hadn't, but she couldn't tell Miss Chichester for she had already flown off. And then Janey had an idea.

"I know what," she said to Joey. "Pin me together." And she pulled the neck part of her costume up over her head. Joey pinned it with two safety pins, and he cut two holes for her eyes. This costume was not comfortable now. Pulling it up and pinning it this way lifted Jane's arms so she had trouble making them hang down the way she thought a bear's should. However, at any rate, she now had a bear head of sorts.

"Do I look like a bear?" she asked Rufus.

"You look like a brown ghost," Rufus replied.

"Don't you worry," said Sylvie, coming up. "You look like a very nice little animal."

"But I'm supposed to be a bear, not a nice little animal," said Jane.

"Well," said Sylvie, "people will know you are supposed to be a bear because Rufus and Joey both have their bear heads on."

So Jane resigned herself to not being a perfect bear. She tried to comfort herself with the thought that she would still be in disguise. She hoped her acting would be so good it would counterbalance her bad head. "Somebody has been eating my porridge," she practiced.

Miss Chichester appeared. "The janitor said 'No,' " she said. She thoughtfully surveyed Jane a moment. "Hm-m-m, a make-shift," she observed. "Well, it's better than nothing," she agreed with Jane. But she decided to switch the order of the program around in order to give everybody one last chance to find the middle bear's real head. She sent Miss Beale out onto the stage. Everybody hoped that while Miss Beale was singing "In an Old-fashioned Garden," the head would appear. But it didn't.

"Keep a little in the background," said Miss Chichester to Jane. "Perhaps people will not notice."

"If I can only see where the background is," thought Jane. For she found it even harder to keep her eyes close to the holes cut in her costume than it had been to the real ones in her regular bear head.

Now the heavy curtain rolled up. It didn't stick halfway up as it sometimes did, and Sylvie, Goldilocks, in a blue pinafore and socks, ran out onto the stage midst loud applause. The play had begun! Sylvie had a great deal of acting to do all by herself before the three bears came home. But she wasn't scared. She was used to being on the stage alone.

Jane's heart pounded as she and Joey and Rufus waited for their cue to come home. If only she didn't trip and turn a somersault, for she really could not see very well. Somehow she managed to see out of only one eye at a time. These eye holes must have been cut crooked. One hole kept getting hooked on her nose.

"Now!" Miss Chichester whispered. "Cue! Out with you three bears."

Joe, Jane, and Rufus, the three bears, lumbered out onto the stage. They were never supposed to just walk, always lumber and lope.

The applause was tremendous. It startled the three bears. The Town Hall was packed. Somebody must have sold a lot of tickets.

"There's Mama," said Rufus. He said it out loud.

He wasn't supposed to say anything out loud except about his porridge, his chair, and his bed. But anyway he said, "There's Mama." Jane could not see Mama. Lumbering out onto the stage had dislocated her costume so that now she could not see at all. Fortunately the footlights shone through the brown flannel of her costume so she could keep away from the edge of the stage and not fall off.

The Moffats all knew their lines so well they

did not forget them once. The only trouble was they did not have much chance to say them because the applause was so great every time they opened their mouths. At last, however, they reached the act about the three beds. An extra platform had been set up on the stage to look like the upstairs of a three bears' house. The three bears lumbered slowly up the steps.

Suddenly shouts arose all over the Hall:

"Her head! Her head! The middle bear's head!"

"Sh-sh-sh," said others. "See what's going to happen."

As Jane could not see very well she had no idea what these shouts referred to. She had the same head on now that she had had on all during this play so far. Why then all these shouts? Or had she really stayed in the background the way Miss Chichester had asked her to, and the audience had only just discovered about the make-shift?

"Oh," whispered Joey to Jane. "I see it. It's your real bear head and it's on the top of my bed post."

"O-o-o-h!" said Jane. "Get it down."

"How can I?" said Joe. "With all these people watching me?"

"Try and get it when you punch your bed," urged Jane.

Joey was examining his big bear's bed now. "Hm-m-m," he said fiercely. "Somebody has been lying on my bed. . . ." But he couldn't reach the middle bear's head. He did try. But he couldn't quite reach it, and there was more laughter from the audience.

Jane pulled her costume about until she could see through the eyehole. Ah, there was her head! On the post of the big bear's bed. No wonder people were laughing. What a place for the middle bear's head. Here she was, without it. And there it was, without her. Jane resolved to get it. Somehow or other she would rescue her head before this play was completely over. Now was her chance. It was her turn to talk about her bed. Instead, Jane said:

"Somebody has been trying on my head, and there it is!"

Jane hopped up on Joey's bed. She grabbed her middle bear head.

"Yes," she repeated. "Somebody has been trying on my head," but as she added, "and here it is!" the safety pins that held her make-shift head together popped open. The audience burst into roars of laughter as Janey's own real head emerged. Only for a second though. For she clapped her middle bear head right on as fast as she could, and hopped off the bed. Goodness, she thought, I showed my real face and I didn't have any paint on it.

Unfortunately Jane still could not see, for she had stuck her bear head on backwards. But the audience loved it. They clapped and they stamped. Bravo! Bravo! Bravo, middle bear! Big boys at the back of the hall put their fingers in their mouths and whistled. And it was a long, long time before Jane could say:

"Somebody has been sleeping in my bed," and the play could go on. At last Rufus discovered Goldilocks in his little bed, and she leaped out of the window. That was the end of the play, and the curtain rolled down.

When the bowing began, Miss Chichester tried to send Jane in backwards, thinking the back of her was the front of her. Fortunately, Rufus held Jane by one paw, and Joey held the other. So she didn't get lost. And the three bears lumbered dizzily on and off many times, sometimes with Sylvie, and sometimes alone. And somebody yelled for "The mysterious middle bear!" It must have been the oldest inhabitant.

Miss Chichester turned Jane's head around for

this bow and at last Jane really did look like a perfect middle bear. Furthermore, she could see out. There was Mama, laughing so hard the tears were rolling down her cheeks. And there was Nancy Stokes with all the Stokes, and Olga was there. And there was Mr. Buckle beaming up at the stage. Jane bowed and lumbered off the stage. She felt good now. Acting was fun, she thought, especially if you could be disguised in a bear uniform. And this time she had not turned a somersault across the stage as she had the time she was a butterfly. True, she had lost her head. But she had found it. And the show had gone on, the way people say shows always do.

Moreover, the Moffats had nice warm bear

pajamas to sleep in for the rest of the winter. Of course they didn't go to bed with the bear heads on. But the rest of the costumes were nice and warm.

8

ECLIPSE OVER CRANBURY

Jane stood on the porch anxiously scanning the sky. There was going to be an eclipse of the sun and she certainly hoped she was not going to miss it.

It seemed to Jane that in the past she had missed a great many important things. For instance, one day there had been a slight earthquake. Oh, it was very slight, just a tremor in

fact, but still it was an earthquake and Jane would have liked to have felt it. However, when the earth quaked she was at the moving pictures with Nancy Stokes. No one in the moving picture house had felt the earthquake, but when Janey got home everybody was talking about it.

Of course a lot of people didn't know it was an earthquake until they read about it in the evening *Register*. Many people thought it was just men blasting on the head of the Sleeping Giant or an explosion somewhere. Mama said the dishes had rattled on the sideboard and Madame-the-bust had swayed on her pedestal.

Jane was sorry she had missed it and for many days afterwards she had gone around with her eyes glued to the ground, looking vainly for cracks in the earth. Or she would fasten her ear to the ground, Indian fashion, hoping to hear a rumble.

But this eclipse now, how could she miss it? Somehow or another, everybody knew about it in advance. For weeks the teacher had talked of little else in school. Everybody knew exactly when to expect it. Nobody knew about the earthquake in advance. Natural to miss it. Just like shooting stars. Of course Jane saw plenty of good shooting stars, but she had an idea she missed the best ones. She'd be reading a book on a warm summer's evening and in would rush Rufus or Joey.

"Boy, oh, boy, you should see the shooting star I just saw!"

The way they told it made Jane envision a star that shot across the sky from horizon to horizon. Her shooting stars were wonderful, but she really never saw anything like the ones they described.

Another important thing which Jane had missed

was the geyser on the corner of Pleasant Street. A water main burst in front of the oldest inhabitant's house and water shot up in the air forty feet! Just like Yellowstone Park, Joey said. Jane wished she'd seen that, but she and Nancy were bathing a stray dog and didn't know about the geyser until there was nothing left but a trickle of water in the gutter.

But the worst thing that might happen was that she might not even know the eclipse *was* the eclipse right while it was going on. It might be like the man in the moon. All of her life she had heard of this man in the moon. But for years she had not been able to find him. She knew the lady in the moon very well. However, the man in the moon was much more famous. Jane always looked for him, expecting a man, well-dressed, with perhaps a tall hat and a cane.

Of course she did see a jolly pie-face. But surely that could not possibly be *the man* the whole world talked about. That's what she had thought anyway until last night when she was walking home from the play in the Town Hall with Mama.

It was nice to be walking home with Mama. They looked at the stars and the moon together. Jane resolved to find out about this man in the moon once and for all.

"I'll give myself until we get to Ashbellows Place," she decided. "If I don't find him by then, I'll ask Mama."

She scrunched along in the snow, happily, with Mama. Mama was telling her about things when she was little in New York.

"... that year we were living in a house that looked out over the East River," Mama was saying. But Janey only half listened while she studied the moon hard. There was the lovely lady in the moon, the same as always. Then, if she blinked her eyes and looked again, there was the jolly pie-face. But the man! Where was he? The man with the top hat and cane?

They reached the corner of Ashbellows Place and still Jane did not see the man in the moon, although her eyes were strained from the effort. She lisened politely until Mama finished her story. Then she said:

"Mama."

"Yes, Janey?"

"You see the moon?"

"Yes, Janey."

"You see the man in the moon?"

"Yes, of course I do, Jane. He's right there for the whole world to see."

"Oh . . ."

Jane fell silent for a moment. For the whole world to see. Why didn't she see him then? If she told Mama she didn't see him, would Mama think she was an ignoramus? Well, ignoramus or not, tonight she was going to find out. She tucked her hand tightly in Mama's, took a deep breath, and then said as though it were a huge joke:

"Well, I don't see him, Mama."

Mama was lost in her own thoughts and did

not answer. She thinks I am an ignoramus, Jane decided.

"Not tonight anyway," she added to ease the blow. "Of course I see the lady in the moon," she went on hastily. "But the man in the moon? . . . No!"

She said this "no" defiantly. All right. She was an ignoramus.

"The man in the moon? No?" Mama repeated absentmindedly. Then, thinking this was a game Jane was playing, she said, "Well, you may not see him. But I see him. The same jolly old fellow I've known all my life."

These words "jolly old fellow" sounded so endearing, Jane did wish she knew him too.

"What does he look like?" she asked.

They stopped under the lamp light. On the snow Mama drew a moon with a face in it. It was a jolly pie-face, the same as Jane saw.

"There," said Mama. "The man in the moon!"

"Oh," gasped Jane. "Is *that* the man in the moon?"

"Of course that's the man in the moon."

"Is that the man in the moon the whole world sees?"

"Yes, Janey."

"Why, I know him," Jane said scornfully, as

though the man in the moon had been putting something over on her.

"Of course you know him," said Mama.

" 'Course I know him," laughed Jane. What a relief! She wasn't an ignoramus. There wasn't any man in the moon with a top hat and cane. Just this jolly pie-face. He was *the man* in the moon.

Now Jane hoped she would not have the same trouble recognizing the eclipse as she had the man in the moon. She looked at the sun, squinting her eyes. Maybe the eclipse was beginning. It wasn't supposed to begin for a couple of hours. Still she wanted to make sure she wasn't going to miss it.

But then, how could she miss it? Jane broke off an icicle from the hop vine and sucked it. Pooh! She couldn't miss it. Not after all those

pictures the teacher had drawn on the blackboard. Jane jumped off the porch and began
drawing pictures of the eclipse in the snow. The
teacher had said, "When the eclipse is total,
then you will see the corona. Look for it. A crown
of fire." Apparently from the way the teacher
spoke, this was going to be one of the biggest
eclipses ever. Scientists and astronomers were
coming from all the world to watch this one
right in New Haven. Because of all the places in
the world New Haven was the best place to
watch it. And Cranbury, being so near, was just
as good.

Since people were coming from Honolulu and
the other side of the earth to see this eclipse,
Jane was beginning to think perhaps she should
go somewhere special to see the eclipse too. Not
just watch it from her own front yard.

"Take a piece of smoked glass and look!" the
teacher had said.

She had not said *go* anywhere and look. Just
look. All the same it began to seem to Jane that
it might be a very good idea to go to some
important spot in Cranbury and look. Like the
top of Shingle Hill. But there was so much snow
on the ground it would be hard to get up there.
What about the tip end of Cranbury, Gooseneck

Point, that jutted out into the harbor? A long flat sand bar, covered now with snow and ice. There, Jane thought, she would really feel she was seeing something important.

She wondered where Joey and Rufus were. Maybe they would go with her. At this moment Rufus staggered out of the back yard with two huge squares of corrugated paper tied to his shoes.

"Just like snowshoes," he muttered, climbing over the embankment of snow at the side of the walk.

"Rufus," said Jane. "Where are you goin' to look at the eclipse?"

"Me and Joey are goin' to look through Wallie Bangs' telescope."

"Oh . . ." Jane was impressed. Like the scientists. She was disappointed, though, because she wanted someone to go with her to Gooseneck Point.

Well, here was Sylvie coming out of the house with a piece of smoked glass in her hand. Maybe she would go with Janey. But no.

"Our science teacher is taking our class up on the roof of the high school. We're going to look through his telescope," said Sylvie.

"Oh . . ." said Jane. More telescopes. She didn't want to be bothered with telescopes and such paraphernalia. These things did not last long, these eclipses. You had to look fast. Anybody might miss the eclipse while they were getting their eyes used to looking through a telescope. Once Mrs. Stokes had taken her and Nancy to see the great dancer, Pavlowa. Mrs. Stokes let Jane look through her little pearl opera glasses. But by the time she got her eyes adjusted to see anything, Pavlowa had left the stage. Furthermore Jane saw that what she had thought were real pine trees was nothing but painted card-board. Better without glasses.

Well, it was lucky she had a best friend. Per-haps Nancy would go with her. Jane went into the house to fix her rubbers and shoes before going on the long walk. Thank goodness, the hole in her rubbers was in the heel and the hole in her shoes was in the toe. The snow would have a harder time working into her stockings than if the holes were in the same spot. She warmed her hands over the kitchen fire.

Joe was smoking pieces of glass to look through. Jane carefully took two of these and then she went into the dining room to kiss Mama good-by. She felt as though she were starting on a long trip.

"Don't get too cold," Mama said, pinching her cheeks and pulling her collar tight around her neck.

"No," said Jane. "Good-by." And she ran through the kitchen waving a good-by to Joey too.

"Where are you goin'?" Joe asked.

"To the eclipse!" Jane yelled, and ran out the door.

She looked at the sky. The sun was still round and whole. She hoped Nancy would go with her.

But she hoped that if she did they would not see any stray dogs on the way. Then, instead of going to the eclipse, they would probably have to come home, bathe, and feed the dog. They would miss the eclipse, the way they had the geyser in front of the oldest inhabitant's house.

"Do you want to go to Gooseneck Point to see the eclipse?" she asked Nancy.

Nancy was delighted. "Sure," she said. "And there might be a blizzard, and we might get lost in it."

Adventure! That's what Nancy liked. She and Jane picked their way through the snow. Nancy had her arctics on.

"Step in my footsteps," she told Jane. "So you won't get snow in your shoes."

If only we don't meet any dogs, prayed Jane. Or horses. Nancy always spent a great deal of time stroking a horse's nose and examining him critically to see that he was well fed and well treated. Jane kept her eyes open for horses and dogs. If she saw one, she pointed at a cloud in the sky to divert Nancy's attention.

They hurried down the street. Wherever the snow was cleared away Janey made Nancy run.

"Hey," remonstrated Nancy. "After all we can really see this eclipse from anywhere."

This was true, but Jane's heart was set on Gooseneck Point. This was the very best place to look at this eclipse, she was sure. Maybe there would be a lot of other people there. Maybe some of the scientists from across the world would be gathered there. That wouldn't surprise Jane one bit. She glanced at the sun. It was still the same sun. Nothing was happening yet.

They turned into Second Avenue. A bright yellow trolley came along.

"How are those people on the trolley goin' to see the eclipse?" asked Jane.

"Perhaps the motorman will stop the trolley for a while so they can all take a look," suggested Nancy.

"I'm afraid they'll all miss it," said Jane. "These motormen have to be a certain place by a certain time. Of course if he hurries and

gets ahead of schedule, maybe he can stop for a few minutes," she decided.

But goodness! There was a little dog across the street.

"Hey!" shouted Jane. "There's a cloud up there. Do you think it will spoil the eclipse?"

"Of course not," said Nancy. "It's miles from the sun."

The cloud got them safely past that dog. Jane breathed a sigh of relief.

"Another thing is this," said Jane. "The sun and the snow are so bright I see spots and circles in front of my eyes. We might get snow-blind and think the eclipse has come, and all the while the darkness will really be our snow-blindedness . . ."

Nancy burst out laughing at this. Ha-ha! That good way she laughed. Like a firecracker going off. Jane had to laugh too. But, there! Another dog! A little brown one coming around that house! It didn't look like a stray dog to Jane, but you couldn't tell how Nancy would feel about it. All dogs, unless she knew them well, like Bosie the fireman's dog, looked stray and hungry to Nancy.

"There's another cloud," she yelled, pointing frantically at the heavens.

"Oh," said Nancy. "It's the same one. Stop worrying about clouds."

Safe again, thought Jane. But not for long! For here, running around the corner, dragging a broken rope from his collar, came a little bedraggled poodle, running right towards them.

"Another cloud," said Jane, grabbing Nancy's arm. But clouds would not help her now. Nancy had seen the dog. Naturally she could not help seeing this dog since it was running right straight towards them.

"Oh, Jane," said Nancy. "The poor little thing! Lost and hungry. Come here, pup," she coaxed.

The little dog turned around and ran up the street in front of them, his tail between his legs. Nancy raced after him.

Jane felt like crying.

"He doesn't look hungry," she yelled, following her best friend. "You can't see any ribs," she added.

"He's lost and hungry," insisted Nancy. "His rope's broken. Maybe he was stolen and just got away. He doesn't know where he is. Nice warm bath . . ."

Now Jane wondered if they would ever get to the tip end of Cranbury. Or would they have to take the dog home to Nancy's house, bathe and feed it, hunt for the owner, and miss the eclipse of the sun?

Fortunately at the present moment the dog was running in the direction of Gooseneck Point. At least, so far, nothing had been lost. If he only doesn't turn around and go the other way, thought Jane.

Jane was a fast runner, and her feet were not weighted down with arctics as Nancy's were. So now she outstripped Nancy, running after the dog. But instead of coaxing him with, "Here, pup! Here, pup!" the way Nancy did, she kept saying, "Shoo! Shoo! Run away, puppy."

She was chasing him right down Second Avenue in the direction she wanted to go.

"Catch him! Catch him!" shouted Nancy. "Don't let the poor pup get away."

"Run! Run!" said Jane to the little dog. For she was sure this little dog was neither lost, strayed, nor stolen, but just happy to be running around loose for once. He had a wellfed look about him. Not a rib was visible.

Now they were all racing down the street toward the end of Second Avenue. There were fewer and fewer houses. And here at last, jutting out into the harbor, was Gooseneck Point! Now the only house they could see was the watchman's house at the very tip end. The going was easier here The wind had swept away most of the soft new snow and left a hard icy crust to walk on.

And the little dog half slid and half ran right out on Gooseneck Point.

"You'd think he had decided to watch the eclipse from Gooseneck Point too," Jane said to Nancy.

But just then Jane broke through the crusty snow. In went one leg up to the knee!

"Too bad we don't have snowshoes," she laughed, thinking of Rufus' cardboard ones.

"Don't worry. I'll catch him," said Nancy.

This is just what Jane hoped Nancy would not do. But suddenly, ahead of her, she saw Nancy sprawl on the snow, slide the way a baseball player does at the plate, and there! she had the dog's rope in her hands.

"She's caught him," moaned Jane.

She examined the sun through her smoked glass. If only the eclipse would begin now, Nancy would wait until it was over to take the dog home and bathe him. But there was no sign of the eclipse so far.

Nancy was having a hard time with this dog. He did not want to turn around and start towards town. Nancy tried to pull him back towards Second Avenue. No, he would not go. He tried to grip his paws in the crusty snow, he scrunched himself up in a little ball, and he almost slipped his head out of his collar. He wanted, apparently, to just keep on going out on Gooseneck Point. Jane's heart warmed to him. He wants to see the eclipse too, she decided.

"This dog does not like to walk on the leash," said Nancy.

He certainly did not. He gasped and choked and snorted and would not yield an inch.

"Perhaps he wants to see the eclipse?" suggested Jane.

"What does a dog know about eclipses? Look! He's shivering. Poor little thing. He's so cold and hungry."

Jane said, "Maybe he will come for me?"

She took the rope and she started walking. But she did not try to persuade the dog to walk nicely back towards Second Avenue. She kept going right out on the point. The little dog did not seem to mind in the least going in this direction. In fact his tail wagged happily.

"He wants to go this way," yelled Jane.

"Well, we might as well go along with him then," said Nancy. "He'll get used to us, and after a while he will go wherever we say."

"And we can all see the eclipse," said Jane joyfully.

"Oh . . . yes . . . I'd almost forgotten," said Nancy.

My, it was deserted out here! And the thin curl of smoke coming out of the watchman's house only added to the loneliness. Jane and Nancy could see the watchman's footsteps frozen in a straight line in the snow to and from his house. Also the footsteps of a cat, or a dog.

"Don't you think it's funny," said Jane, "that nobody else thought of coming here to watch the eclipse except us?"

"Nobody else had the bravery," said Nancy.

"Of course," continued Jane, "you wouldn't expect scientists from Honolulu to know about this spot. But I am surprised that everybody in Cranbury isn't here."

"Just lazy, I suppose," said Nancy.

Jane and Nancy found themselves whispering. All of a sudden it seemed more quiet and still than before. It was so quiet their ears hurt, the way they did in church sometimes. Jane was certainly glad that Nancy had come with her. She would have felt too little if she were here alone. The sea-gulls circled about, their wings catching the glint of the sun. Suddenly they all swooped to earth and settled on the ice, all facing the same direction, like so many Moslems at prayer. The little dog whined and shivered.

"I should think that eclipse would begin now," said Jane, stamping up and down. Ouch! Her feet were getting so cold! Why couldn't the sun eclipse now so they could go home? They were ready. The sun was ready. Everything was ready. Here they were at Gooseneck Point with smoked glass. Supposing the papers had gotten the day wrong. If they had, all those famous scientists who had come from the ends of the earth would be pretty angry.

"Begin, eclipse!" Jane shouted.

This made Nancy laugh and startled the sea-gulls into circling around.

"Begin, eclipse," they both shouted. They waved their arms and even the little dog barked and wagged his tail.

But then everybody fell silent again. In the middle of winter this really was no place for hilarity. Different from the summer time when there were picnics, laughing, and swimming on this Point. But now it was too lonesome. The sea-gulls settled morosely down again, and the little dog stood with bent head, and eyes turned in the direction of the watchman's house.

Well, surely it must be time now. Jane and Nancy stared at the sun. Was it beginning? Was this thin shadow on the edge of the sun the beginning?

"It's beginning! It's beginning!" shouted Nancy.

"Beginning . . ." echoed Jane.

She saw it too. She saw the eclipse. She saw it and she knew she was seeing it! The shadow grew larger and larger. Now the sun looked as though someone had bitten a chunk out of it. Now it was half covered and the light was strange and dim. Slowly the moon spread its shadow across the sun and finally the sun was blotted out entirely. Eclipse of the sun! That's what that was.

"Now there's the corona," said Nancy. "Just like the teacher said."

"M-m-m," said Jane. "But I thought it was going to be red."

Still, red or not, she saw the corona. She saw the eclipse and she saw the corona. So far she had not missed any of it. Jane wondered if the lady in the moon felt happy to be blotting out the big sun for once. It's good she does this once in a while, Jane thought. Otherwise who would know the sun had a corona to it?

But now the sun was coming out on the other side. Soon there it was, all whole again. The eclipse of the sun was over! It did not last awfully long. Jane hoped all those scientists and astronomers who had come from the ends of the earth would not be disappointed. She was glad it was over now though, for her feet were so cold!

"Well," said Nancy. "Come on, pup! We'll give you a good dinner. That's what you need."

The little dog shook himself hard, as though he had just had a bath or come in from a swim. Then, giving a sudden lurch, he broke loose. With his rope dangling behind him he bounded down the sand bar. When he had almost reached the watchman's house he turned around and barked gaily at the two girls.

"Oh," exclaimed Jane, "I bet he's the watchman's dog."

"Oh, of course," said Nancy. And at this moment the watchman came out of his house and whistled. "That's just who he does belong to. He does need a bath, though."

Then the two girls burst out laughing. Now that the eclipse was over it felt all right, good in fact, to laugh. Supposing they had taken the dog home, bathed and fed him, and all the while he belonged right here. Then they would have missed the eclipse all for nothing, the eclipse that people had come across the earth to see.

They turned and left Gooseneck Point. Jane sighed. The eclipse of the sun was over and they hadn't missed any of it. They hadn't had to bathe a dog. When the Moffats were all sitting around the table that night, they would all talk about it, and she would have seen every bit of it! And from what a place! Gooseneck Point. With no paraphernalia, but still, like the scientists, she had gone to the eclipse. She had not just watched it from her own front yard.

"O-o-o-h, come on!" said Nancy. "I'm so hungry."

"Me too. And ouch! My chilblains hurt!" said Jane. And they hurried home.

9

JANEY TAKES UP SPORTS

When the new parish house was built, there was a splendid gymnasium added to it. Sometimes when Janey was sitting on the Green, resting from a hike up on Shingle Hill and watching the ants, she could hear the junior girls' basketball team practicing. She could hear the umpire's shrill whistle, the yelling and shouting and stamping of the players, and the ball bouncing across

the floor or banging against the
wires. It sounded like a lot of
fun. Sometimes Janey thought
she should join the basketball
team and stop watching the
ants.

Here was this lovely new gymnasium with the new plaster
smell to it, and none of the
Moffats belonged! It seemed too
bad. When the new gymnasium
was finished, the minister in the
pulpit had said:

"The gymnasium belongs to you. To all of you.
Use it and rejoice that we now have such a
splendid gymnasium for our young people."

Whenever Janey saw the minister, she felt self-
conscious to think that none of the Moffats, not
one of them, belonged to the gymnasium. He
would think the Moffats did not appreciate it.
They all four belonged to the library, all four
went to school, went to Sunday School, and dancing school too, except Rufus. Yet none of them
belonged to the gymnasium. Well, as for Sylvie,
she simply did not have the time, that was all
there was to that—graduating in June, practicing
her solos, her dancing and singing. And Joey! He

was so busy too. He was always having to deliver papers, take care of furnaces, sift ashes and mow lawns. When would they have the time for

the new gymnasium? As for Rufus, he was too little. Besides right now very likely you couldn't tear him away from his and Joey's wireless set. That left her, Jane, the middle Moffat. If she joined, that would make one out of four at least. She should join.

"... A splendid gymnasium for our young people," murmured Jane, remembering the words of the minister.

She, Janey, was one of the young people and she had set foot in the new gymnasium only once, the night of the parish house apple blossom bazaar.

"I should join," she thought. Today was a very warm day in the early spring. She lazily watched a big, black ant pushing and tugging at a mutilated beetle. Now and then from across the Green the wind carried the voices of the high school chorus practicing the graduation music. Sylvie was there. They were singing "Hail, Bright Abode." It was pretty. After a while they began to practice "Alan-a-dale." Jane said to herself again, "I should join. Yes, I should."

There was one drawback. Nancy didn't belong. But Nancy had her music lessons and Jane didn't. To even things up Janey could join the basketball team. Nancy would go off to practice her music. Janey would go off to practice her basketball. Right now some of the basketball girls had come out onto the Green to rest. They were dressed in white middy blouses and bloomers. They all wore sneakers on their feet.

Janey loved sneakers. She had hers on today too. She could run like lightning in them and always beat the trolley cars except the Bridgeport Express. Almost like flying. She didn't have any of those big bloomers. But maybe Mama would make her a pair out of the blue serge skirt she had torn jumping over the back fence.

Should she join? She pondered this question. She considered other sports. At most games of ball she was none too good. She might as well be honest about that. Joey would seldom play ball with her, preferring little Rufus even, unless there was absolutely no one else around. At croquet she was pretty good. She rarely finished first; but also she rarely finished last. Once in a fit of exuberance over having won she had thrown the croquet ball straight up in the air. She looked for it to catch it. She didn't see it and thought she must have thrown it right up into the blue sky where it would probably make a hole and there would be a new sun. Suddenly it came down! Ouch! Right on her head and raised quite

a lump. It had staggered her but she had walked off in silent dignity when Rufus said in disgust:

"Oh, Jane! Can't you catch anything?"

Jane had an idea these tremendous basketballs would be easier to catch. You could encircle them with your whole body and hug.

As far as other sports went, she couldn't swim yet but she was going to learn this summer. She could do the dead man's float. She could do it with her eyes open and see the shells and the crabs crawling on the bottom. But she wasn't sure that was a sport. And she was really a wonderful runner and running was good for basketball. A couple of times Janey had watched the basketball team practice in school. They certainly did a lot of running to and fro. Now and then someone seemed to get the ball in the basket. That was good. When someone got the ball in the basket, everybody yelled. Basketball, that's what that was.

"I should join." Jane blissfully pictured herself tossing the ball through the basket as easily as flipping tiddledywinks into the cup. She would win the game and be carried on the other girls' shoulders like the heroes in the Barbour books that Joey was always reading. At the last moment when her side was losing and the game seemed to be lost, she would slip in sidewise, flip the ball up, and it would fall clean through. The game would be saved and, "Hurrah for Jane Moffat!" everybody would yell. Her side had won, thanks to her cunning.

More exciting still, the ball would land on the rim of the basket, teeter back and forth for several seconds with all the players on her side willing it in, and she willing the hardest, and all the players on the other side willing it to fall outside. But of course in a breath-taking moment the ball would slide in and again, "Hurrah for Janey Moffat!" everybody would yell.

These were very pleasant thoughts. Jane turned over on her back, stared vacantly at the clouds and wondered why she had not considered joining the basketball team sooner. It was rather late in the season, but possibly by joining now she would save the team from a season of disgrace. This sometimes happened in the Barbour books.

The girls went back into the gymnasium, the umpire's whistle blew shrilly, and there was a loud burst of shouting. An exciting moment! "Yes, I s'pose I should join," said Jane. She rubbed the bits of grass and clover off her skirt and legs and crossed the street.

She pushed open the door into the new parish house. It still smelled of plaster and paint. She tiptoed through the assembly room and skirted the little platform where the minister stood. There was a white sheet tacked on the wall behind this, swaying in the breeze. Here the minister showed his lantern slides of his journey to the Holy Land every Friday evening.

The door that led into the gymnasium was ajar and she went in. Goodness, what a noise! Screaming. Yelling. Bouncing. Banging. Stamping. Jane hugged the side wall and moved cautiously over to the back window which looked out on the car barn.

She leaned her elbows against the window sill and watched the practicing. No one noticed her and she was glad of that. The players were all wrapt in what they were doing. Jane didn't see how any of them could tell what they were doing, though. She thought the idea of the game was to get the ball through the basket. However, they seemed often to miss what looked to Jane like marvelous opportunities to toss it in, but bounced it off somewhere else.

"Oh, I am stupid," muttered Jane. "Of course some are supposed to keep the others from doing what they want to do."

That was the game of it!

Jane was beginning to think that she should read more of the Barbour books and find out what the rules were. And just then the umpire blew her whistle and everything stopped. The girls came over to the side seats and sat around in groups and talked and laughed. All of a sudden someone grabbed Jane around the shoulders. It was Mary Jetting, a girl a class or two ahead of Jane in school. M. J. Her initials were the same as Jane's, only backwards.

"Hello, Jane," she said. "I didn't know you played basketball."

Jane smiled.

"Do you want to join the team?"

Jane smiled again, saying neither yes nor no. She wasn't sure.

"Come on, Jane. Help us out. Midge Egan sprained her ankle, had to drop out. We're in a pickle. Big game with the Congoes in half an hour. We're warmin' up now. How about it?"

Jane smiled again. She felt embarrassed because everybody had gathered around and was staring at her.

"Aw, she's too small," said one big girl.

"She's not," defended Mary Jetting. "She's small. But not too small. She's probably fast and wiry and can dart in and out like an eel. I know her type."

Dart in and out like an eel, thought Jane. She would remember that.

"Can you throw a basket?" asked someone.

Before Jane could answer, someone thrust the huge round basketball into her arms.

"Let's see you throw a basket, Pee-wee," the girl said.

Jane felt too shy to resist and ran out onto the shiny floor.

"I hope it's as easy as tiddledywinks," she thought dubiously.

The ball seemed enormous. She stopped below the basket. She held the ball high above her

head a second, popping off several buttons from her guimpe as she did so. Then she threw the ball with all her strength. Up, up, up, and into the basket. No teetering on edges. A clean throw! Right through the basket!

The girls screamed. They cheered and blew whistles. Jane stood below the basket, embarrassed. She looked down at her sneakers. She was surprised herself. And she was a little proud but she was resolved not to grow puffy or stuck-up about it.

"Where've you *been* all these weeks, Pee-wee?" Mary Jetting asked.

"Just around," replied Jane modestly. She kept wondering to herself whether she had sent that ball through the basket by accident or because she really was good.

The big girl on the team

had the same doubts. "Do it again, Pee-wee," she said implacably.

Jane grabbed the ball again. She hugged it to her and stood under the basket, hoping for the best. She threw the ball again. This time she threw it so hard she broke one of the straps of her suspender dress. But the ball shot up and up and clean through the basket again, as beautifully as the first time. For a moment everybody stood there in silence. Jane was struck dumb herself. Suddenly everybody burst into cheers.

While the girls cheered, Janey again fastened her eyes on her sneakers in modesty, and tried not to smile too hard or seem self-satisfied. Then the team formed in a circle, and keeping up a steady, running gait the players took turns throwing baskets.

Jane got the ball in the basket every time it was her turn to throw.

She didn't understand it herself. Beginner's luck, she decided. While this warming up was going on, the other team, the Congoes, rushed into the gymnasium. With a yip-yippy-yip, they too formed into a circle and started warming up at the other end of the hall.

"Like Indians dancing around the campfire," thought Jane.

Suddenly the umpire blew her shrill whistle. All the girls on both the teams rushed to the middle of the floor. And Jane was part of that yelling, bouncing, whistling, and stamping she had listened to so many times from the Green when she was watching the ants. She had no idea what was going on. Everybody else seemed to know. But she didn't.

There were three things that Jane knew definitely about basketball. One was you tried to get the ball through the basket. Another was you must not run with the ball. Just bounce it where it was going or pass it. Then Mary Jetting had said she could weave in and out like an eel. Weaving in and out like an eel really made three things she knew.

If it were left to Jane she would have preferred to spend the entire time throwing baskets. She was so good at that. She wasn't so good at bouncing. Someone always got the ball away from her. So until she had a chance to throw baskets, she resolved that weaving in and out like an eel would be her contribution to the game. This she proceeded to do.

"The trouble with this game," she thought as she darted here and there, "is that I can't tell my team from their team." All the girls were wearing white middy blouses and dark blue bloomers. There must be some way of telling us all apart, Jane reasoned. But she couldn't stand still long enough to figure it out. And Mary Jetting was the only girl she really knew on her team. All the while Janey was trying to see how you could tell one team from the other, she kept weaving in and out like an eel, fast and wiry, like Mary Jetting had said. She hoped she was doing some good for the right side.

It was very confusing. Especially as some of the girls, Jane assumed they were enemies, occasionally shouted at her, "Hey, kid, get off the floor."

This really embarrassed Jane. She realized she was not dressed properly. Her skirt was tight and had torn at the seams. Her guimpe was sticking out of her skirt. Buttons had popped and her stockings kept falling down.

She wished she could get hold of the ball and throw some baskets. Ah! Ouch! Someone thrust the ball into her stomach, nearly knocking all the breath out of her. Janey's arms automatically closed around the ball. Here was her chance!

She balanced for a second. Then she threw the ball. Up, up, and up! You could almost hear the girls holding their breath. Up and through the

basket. Straight through it. Clean. Hurrah! Score! Everybody yelled. Jane pretended she did not realize the yelling was in her honor.

"It's nothin'," she muttered.

Now the game became wilder. Jane's hair came unbraided and it kept falling into her eyes. It was hard to see and it was hard to have to keep on pulling up her stockings and her petticoat. In spite of these impediments, Jane kept on darting in and out like an eel. She was resolved to play a good game, fast and wiry, to keep her reputation and be a credit to Mary Jetting. Whenever she could she threw a basket.

After a while Jane began to wish she could play a more spectacular part in this game. More baskets! She had thrown three but she wanted more. One every minute. That's what she wanted. Fast and wiry and slipping in and out like an eel was all right as far as it went, and if it were meant to throw consternation into the ranks of the enemy, she was doing the best she could. However, throwing baskets, hearing the cheers! That's what she liked.

"Phew!" she breathed, pushing the hair off her forehead and wiping her brow. She was getting tired. Now she would like to win the game quickly, be acclaimed as a hero, and go home.

She was horrified when Mary Jetting passed her and said desperately, "We got to do better. Score's fourteen to six. Favor of the Congoes."

Gracious! Her side was losing. This would never do. She resolved to stop this weaving in and out like an eel and try to get hold of the ball, throw it through the basket again and again. Get the score up to fourteen at least. But she was so much smaller than most of the other girls that just as she was about to encircle the ball with her arms, somebody came along and bounced it away from her.

"Good work, Pee-wee," Mary Jetting yelled at her once, although she had no idea what she had done. She certainly had not thrown another basket. With a sigh Jane resumed her weaving in and out like an eel. She began to wish that someone else would win the game, be acclaimed as a hero, so they could all go home. She paused for a moment, looked up at the basket, thought practice more fun than the actual game of basketball. And she thought tiddledywinks more fun than practice.

At this moment the whistle blew! The girls yelled! The two teams separated. End of the first half! Janey saw Mary Jetting gather her team in a little circle. Heads close together, legs and feet far apart, the girls looked like a wigwam. The other team did the same. Jane felt left out of things.

"It's probably because I don't have my uniform on," she thought.

Jane took advantage of the lull to braid her hair. She noticed now how you could tell the two teams apart. Mary Jetting and her team had red laces in their middies and the other girls had white ones. Knowing this should be of some help during the rest of the game.

Suddenly her team began chanting:

> A-tisket, A-tasket,
> Who can throw a basket?
> Pee-wee Moffat,
> Pee-wee Moffat,
> Rah!
> Rah!
> Rah!

Each "Rah!" was accompanied by the players' right arms shooting straight up in the air.

"Good going, Pee-wee," said Mary, breaking up the group and patting Jane on the back. "But there's tough going ahead. Fourteen to six! Oh! We just can't lose the championship," she moaned.

"I don't know where we'd be without you, though."

Jane stuck her stomach out, wiggled her toes around inside of her sneakers, and kept her eyes lowered modestly.

"What's three baskets?" she said. She'd try to get a dozen or so for them in the next half. Save the championship.

The umpire blew her whistle. In a flash the shouting, bouncing, yelling, and stamping began again. Jane lingered on the side a moment and then she ran into the melee like a dancer who has received her cue. She darted in and out like an eel just as adroitly as before, but now she kept her eyes on the ball every second. She was going to take a more active part in this half. She wasn't going to wait until someone thrust the ball into her arms. She was going to get hold of it herself. This half there was going to be less weaving in and out like an eel and more throwing baskets, she hoped.

A girl came along bouncing the ball. Janey grabbed for it, bursting her other suspender strap as she did so. She got hold of the ball and she threw it wild. The ball hit the edge of the basket and balanced there a second.

"In, in . . ." urged Janey, making a shoving gesture with her arms as though that would help. She even blew hard. Maybe her breath would make the ball fall on the right side. Whether these things helped or not, it did fall through the basket. But the whistle blew and there was a lot of shouting.

"Foul! Foul!" everybody screamed.

"Foul," thought Jane. How terrible! What had she done? Would they put her off the floor? Instead of a hero on people's shoulders, a maker of fouls, sent home in disgrace!

Mary Jetting ran up to her. "Never mind, Pee-wee," she said. "Even the most famous players get the baskets mixed up sometimes. Just like football players sometimes try to make a touchdown at the wrong goal. We've changed baskets, you know."

Jane was comforted a little but when she saw another point tacked onto her opponent's score, she was very miserable. Fifteen to six now. She must retrieve her reputation.

The whistle blew again. In a flash the game was on, hot and furious. Bouncing, yelling, whistling, screaming all began as though there had never been a lull. Janey began weaving in and out like an eel, being as fast and wiry as possible in order to make up for that foul. She hadn't known it made any difference which basket you got the ball in. She thought any basket would do. It had just been a matter of luck she had thrown it into the right basket in the first place. Well! She was learning a lot.

The trouble was that weaving in and out like an eel was becoming monotonous. To lend variety to this sort of play, Jane tried a private game of "In and out the window." She wove in front of this girl, and behind that. But just baskets! That's what she really liked. Ping! Like a tiddledywink. In the ball went! Then the loud cheers. That was fun.

Jane was getting a little dizzy and she wished she could take time out and fasten her stockings. She bumped into Mary Jetting at this moment.

"Nice going, Pee-wee," said Mary. "But we've got to work fast now. Score's fifteen to fourteen and the game's nearly over."

Fifteen to fourteen! Who got all those other baskets? She must have been dreaming.

Jane wove away from Mary. Fifteen to fourteen! Goodness! Something should be done for Mary Jetting's side. Where was the ball now? She looked around the gymnasium. Oops! Someone was about to throw it into the enemy basket. Jane eeled over to her but was too late to prevent the girl from scoring a basket. Terrible! Now the score was seventeen to fourteen. Jane did not want to see her side lose. But the other team was flushed with victory and yelling, and in a mood like that they could ride the score up higher.

The stamping, yelling, bouncing, and the shrill screams became more excited than ever. The umpire blew her whistle almost constantly. It was really terribly confusing. The worst thing for Jane was the condition her clothes were in.

They simply would not stay together. It was hard to keep them on at all, so many buttons and straps had broken. Never would she play basketball again until she had a real uniform. She was happy to see that the elastic band had broken in some of the others' bloomer legs which flopped about their ankles like pajamas.

Whew! What a game!

Jane tried to concentrate her weaving under her own basket so she would be right there on the spot when the ball came this way and the time came to win the game for her side. Of course a lot of the time the whole bunch of players were out in the middle of the floor or at the other end, and there wasn't anyone for her to dart in and out among. Then she would have to abandon her stronghold under the basket and at least appear to be part of the game. So she'd weave herself back and forth from players to basket and from basket to players, holding herself in readiness.

Suddenly Mary Jetting came bouncing the ball across the floor. She was followed by a stream of yelling, grabbing girls. Mary passed it to Jane. Jane caught it!

"I caught the ball," she yelled in astonishment. Oh, if only Rufus or Joey had seen that!

Who can throw a basket?
Pee-wee Moffat,
Pee-wee Moffat!

Everybody was chanting it. It was a challenge.
Jane threw the ball. Up! Up! Ah, up! Right
through the basket. The cheering was tremendous. But Jane did not heed the cheers. Instead
she ran under the basket, caught the ball as it
fell through, backed out onto the floor, and threw

again! And it fell through again! Well! When the ball soared through the basket this second time, such a roar swelled through the gymnasium that several conductors and motormen rushed out of the car barn with lunch cases in hand, and stuck their elbows into the windows and looked through the side door and cheered too.

The umpire was in a quandary. This was the first game she had ever umpired, for the real umpire was ill. And she didn't know whether a double basket of this sort counted as two scores or not. She quickly got out her little book of rules, both boys' rules and girls' rules, for this team played a little of both. In these books there was no mention of double baskets, either for or against. It seemed to the umpire that a double basket should count as two. Popular opinion, too, was in favor of Janey and a double score, although there were a few dissenting cries from the enemy team. In the end, since it was so unusual a thing, the umpire decided to count it. This made the score eighteen to seventeen in favor of Janey's side. And at this instant the five o'clock whistle blew. The game was over! Eighteen to seventeen! Janey's side had won! Her team chanted:

A-tisket, A-tasket,
Who can throw a basket?
Pee-wee Moffat,
Pee-wee Moffat,
Rah!
Rah!
Rah!

Then they all grabbed Jane and they carried her around the room on their shoulders, cheering and yelling. Jane was very embarrassed. It was better to dream of these things. Besides her clothes were all coming off. Finally they stopped and let her down.

"Would you like to play regular next year?" asked Mary, for this was the last game of the season.

Jane shook her head. "No, thanks," she said. Next year was a long time away and she couldn't promise something so far ahead. Anyway, she had to think it over, whether or not she liked this game. She was very tired. Right now she was inclined to think that she would rather listen to the game from outside while she was sitting on the Green than actually to be in here playing. Of course, all these baskets! They had been fun. But Jane was obliged to admit to herself that they must have been a matter of luck. She looked herself over. What a mess she was in! And, goodness, her guimpe was on inside out! Well, that might explain the luck. Nancy Stokes told her if you put on your clothes inside out by accident, it had to be by accident, you would have good luck.

Mary Jetting was still standing near by. "You could be the captain," she said generously, because she was the captain herself.

"No, thanks," said Jane again. And then, because she did not wish to seem unappreciative, she added, "But I'll ask Mama. It is a lot of fun, especially getting the ball in the basket. Like tiddledywinks."

"Well, thank you, Pee-wee. Think it over. You saved our lives today," said Mary heartily. And she gave Jane a friendly slap on the back again. "So long," she waved.

Jane limped out of the parish house. Someone had stepped on her foot real hard and it hurt. Her face was streaked with dirt and her stockings and clothes were all awry. She pulled up her stockings the best she could and tried to straighten herself out in general, for she saw the minister talking with the sexton near the tulip bed. Then she gave him a friendly nod. Now she could look the minister in the eye. For now she had made use of the splendid new gymnasium, even though, so far, none of the other Moffats had.

10

BEST FRIENDS AGAIN

"Best friends" was over. At least so it seemed to
Jane, for Nancy had not spoken to her in over a
week. She had spoken *at* her—"Jane is a pain"—
but not *to* her. Not since one night during a
game of cops and robbers when Jane had sided
with Beatrice in a dispute, instead of siding with
Nancy.

The dispute arose over a question of boundary. Beatrice had gone past a certain house. Nancy said she should have gone up to that house not past it. "Shouldn't she have, Jane?" And she appealed to Jane for support. Jane had hesitated before an-  swering because she liked to agree with Nancy. Then reluc- tantly she said she thought Beatrice was right. For she did really think so. But Nancy got mad at her and had not spoken since.

Today Jane re- mained in her seat when school was dismissed. The monitor wound up the victrola, the music started, and Jane listened to the class march out. She had decided to stay and help the teacher clap the erasers and so give Nancy plenty of time to get out of sight before she started for home. She could not bear to hear Nancy shout, "Jane is a pain," and see her walk home with a big group of other children instead of with her the way she used to when they were best friends.

First Jane leaned out the window and clapped

the chalky erasers, trying not to get the dust in her nose and eyes. Then she washed the blackboards. One blackboard had a big chart on it where the teacher wrote in chalk the names of all the children who brought the first of any kind of wild flower. Jane wished her name was on the list.

Why was it, she wondered, that she was never the first one? She never got her name on the blackboard with something like this:

JANE M.　　　HEPATICA　　　APRIL 17.

That's the way it would be if she were the first to find hepatica. But she never seemed to be the first to find hepatica or anything else. She had run in this morning with chickweed, only to see that someone else had brought it in just a few seconds before. She would have been content to be the first chickweed finder, or the first jill-in-the-grass finder. Nothing fancy like columbine or lady's-slippers.

Maybe this afternoon she would look in the big lot across the street from home and find something. She and Nancy had been planning many trips to the top of Shingle Hill to look for wild flowers together. It was more fun to look

for wild flowers with someone. Jane blinked back the tears. She hoped that by now Nancy was home.

But she wasn't. When Jane ran out of the schoolhouse, there was Nancy, talking to a group of girls.

"Jane is a pain!" she yelled lustily from the other side of the street. Jane walked home with as much dignity as she could muster, cheeks burning. Of course she had to go home the long way. Now she could not take the short cut through the little gate in Nancy's fence.

"Jane is a pain," she muttered. "I am not!" she angrily denied.

Jane felt cross and miserable, and it did not help her to feel better when Mama asked her to sweep down the stairs. Sweeping the stairs, dusting, washing dishes! These were Jane's regular jobs. Now she tramped up the stairs with the dustpan and brush. She made a big clatter and she skipped all the corners. In fact she was through in just a couple of minutes.

When she went into the dining room Mama was basting together a new middy blouse for her.

"Why do you baste first?" Jane asked. "When I sew for my dolls, I just sew, I don't baste first."

"Well," said Mama, "a good sewer bastes first. And I always say it's better to try and do a good job, or at least do the best you can, no matter what the job is. Otherwise what's the sense of doing it at all?"

Jane was silent. She wiggled her toes around

in her shoes, feeling slightly guilty about the stairs. She went back and looked at them. Why do a job at all unless you do a good one? She certainly had done a terrible job on the stairs. Should she do them over? Well ... tomorrow she would do them right. She would not leave even one tiny, teeniest speck of dirt in the corners. She would get something as little as a paint brush and get out every single speck from every corner.

After dinner, when all the dishes were washed and dried and put away, Jane sat down on the top step of the little square porch. It was quite dark now. Daylight was gone. Tomorrow they were going to begin saving daylight. Daylight saving time. And how could they save daylight, Jane wondered? When she first heard about saving daylight she had thought, "What a wonderful idea!" She envisioned an enormous storage box where the daylight could be saved and let out bit by bit as needed, particularly during the cold winter afternoons when an extra bit of daylight would come in very handy. If the gas meter ran out, and the Moffats did not have a quarter in the house, and the oil for the lamps was gone, all they would have to do would be to let a little daylight out of the box.

However, that was not what daylight saving time meant. It meant pushing the clock ahead an hour, calling it four o'clock when it was really three. Mama said this too saved quarters. But Jane was disappointed there would be no big box of daylight.

Even so, tomorrow daylight saving time began. It was an important day. Maybe it was as important as New Year's Day. Jane wondered if Nancy thought so.

If she did, she might make a resolution, the

way people did for New Year's, to stop being
mad at Janey Moffat, to stop yelling "Jane is a
pain," and to start being best friends again.

Was "best friends" going to be over for good?
Jane frowned back her tears. No more cops and
robbers, or hide-and-go-seek, and playing in the
house with the slippery floors?

Jane listened to the shouts that came from
Nancy Stokes' yard. Over there all the children
were having a good game of hide-and-go-seek.

"Any-body-roun'-my-goal-is-it!" Jane heard
Nancy yell.

Jane swallowed hard. But goodness! She should
be getting used to having Nancy not speaking to
her any more.

"All in! All in!" She heard Nancy's voice again.

Jane stared at the sky. There was no moon
tonight, but millions and millions of stars press-
ing into the sky! The harder Jane looked, the
more stars seemed to try to elbow into the heavens. So many stars!

Jane closed her eyes. She put her head in her
lap. What a perfect night for a game like hide-
and-go-seek or cops and robbers with Nancy
Stokes.

Usually Nancy was right. Why not go over
there now and say she thought Nancy was right

after all that night? Then they could be best friends again. But she couldn't do that because

in the first place it wasn't so. She didn't think Nancy was right that time.

"Beef-steak! Beef-steak!" she heard the children yell.

Jane cupped her chin in her hands and looked at the sky. "Please let Nancy think daylight saving time day is like New Year's and let her make a resolution not to be mad at me any more," said Jane.

Someone came scuffling up the walk. It was

Joey. Sparks flew out in the night from his heavy shoes.

"Hello," he said. "Gee, some night, isn't it?"

"M-m-m," said Jane.

"Come home! Come home! Wherever you are!" they heard the children yell.

"Sounds like a good game," said Joe. "Don't you want to play?"

"No!" said Jane defiantly.

Joe first stamped his feet to shake off some of the ashes from the oldest inhabitant's cellar. Although tonight was a soft warm spring evening, he had made a little fire just to take the chill off the house. Then Joey went indoors. Some of the sounds and the light inside came out for a second, and then it was darker and more lonely than ever outside.

"Come home! Come home! Wherever you are!" Jane heard Nancy's voice again. It was louder and clearer than anybody's. Suppose she went over and "ran in," and pretended that she had been playing all the while. But no. Nancy would yell, "Jane is a pain."

Maybe she should get a new best friend. Clara Pringle? Once or twice lately she had played with Clara. But Clara did not have the bravery Nancy had.

Or perhaps she should begin to live the way she used to live before she ever had a best friend, before she knew Nancy at all. Then there were just the four Moffats. There was always Joe or Rufus or Sylvie, or all three, to play with. Now everything was different.

Look at Sylvie! Practically a grown-up, graduating from high school soon, the valedictorian. And besides that she got love letters, you might as well call them that, from some red-headed sailor who had not even set eyes on her since they were in Room Four together. Now when he was way out at sea, he remembered her long curls. Sylvie hardly remembered him. But she liked to get his letters. Naturally . . . She was sweet sixteen.

Sometimes Jane watched Sylvie in amazement. Here was Sylvie apparently quite happy in spite of having her hair done up, her skirts a funny length, neither long nor short, and never a game of Indians in the empty lot! Maybe she didn't know she was a grown-up. Or maybe she liked doing the things she did now, just as much as Janey liked playing hide-and-go-seek with Nancy Stokes.

Suddenly Jane stood up. Maybe she, Janey, was growing up and not doing things any more that she used to love to do. But she couldn't think of anything. For instance, she still raced trolley cars, played Indians, cops and robbers. . . . Yes, she was still the same, thank goodness!

She stooped over and looked from between her legs, upside-down, at the houses with their bright lights shining in the windows and at the tall elm tree that disappeared into the sky. Everything looked so clear and neat, the way things always did the upside-down way. But wait! Jane popped right side up again with a start.

Here was something she didn't do any more that she used to do so often—look at things the upside-down way. She just almost never thought to do this any more. Not since the Moffats had moved into this little white house. She had been so busy with Nancy Stokes, being her best friend, and doing all she could to help the oldest inhabitant reach the age of one hundred, she just hadn't thought to do this. Maybe she had grown up some too, and she hadn't even known it.

Maybe growing up wasn't as bad as it seemed, because you were so busy doing what you were doing, you didn't miss the things you used to do. After all, she didn't play blocks or make mud pies any more. And she didn't miss them. And there was a time when she probably thought mud pies and blocks were very nice things.

But if Janey should try to live the way she used to before she had a best friend, she couldn't spend all her time looking at things the upside-down way. And Sylvie was too busy to play with her. What about Joey and Rufus now? Dot-da-dot-dot! Tuning in! Tuning in all the time on their radio.

Even at this very moment a light shone out of the window of their little front bedroom where they had built their set. The minute he came in Joey had gone upstairs to tune in. Rufus too.

Jane looked through the hop vines up to their window. The two boys were sitting there with their ear phones on. Their window was wide open. This was so they could yell at Wallie Bangs who was sitting in his back bedroom window with his brother Eddie, tuning in also.

Of course Wallie and Eddie couldn't tune in as often as Joey and Rufus because Wallie very frequently took their radio apart. Tonight however both radios were working.

"Did you hear that?" one boy would yell.

"Yeh, Arlington time signal."

"No . . . not quite time for that yet . . ."

Perhaps she too should go up and be interested in the radio, thought Jane. Radio! When Jane first heard about this new thing, radio, which had just been invented, she was very excited. Everybody was talking about it. Even Nancy Stokes. But Nancy said her family was going to wait and get one when they were perfected. Not Joey and Rufus

though. They were going to perfect theirs right now. They were going to hear things, right here in the Moffats' own house, that were going on in Boston, and lots of other places. No wires like the telephone. Wire*less*. Soon they were going to hear everything that went on all over the world.

Joey and Rufus made their set out of an old quart-size ice-cream container. Joey saved the money he received for dusting the pews for the sexton of the church every Saturday morning. Finally he had enough to buy two pairs of ear phones. Joey and Rufus talked excitedly about the radio all the time, and they used a lot of words that Jane had never heard before. Crystal of galena, they talked about most of the time. This crystal of galena sounded good to Jane. Like the Arabian Nights. A gazing bowl. Not only hearing what was going on in Boston, but crystal gazing as well. When she saw the crystal she was quite disappointed. A tiny thing! Not at all like a gazing bowl. Once in a while Joey or Rufus asked her if she'd like to listen. They put the ear phones on her head and she listened hard. Then she told her brothers she would wait until they played music instead of these strange sounds. However she had never heard the Arlington time signal. That might be nicer.

Yes, she might take up radio now that she had the time. It must be fun or Joey and Rufus would not spend every second they had tuning in. They even plugged the keyhole and the cracks around the door with cotton and newspapers so they could listen in for the Arlington time signal in the middle of the night. They were both late to school nearly every day now. Rufus was forgetting to carry the one in arithmetic more than ever. And all winter Joey had shamefully neglected the oldest inhabitant's furnace. He had let the fire go out all too often.

This horrified Jane. The oldest inhabitant! The most important man in Cranbury! He might catch cold, and all because of Joey's radio.

Jane listened. In the still night air she could hear the static. Now it was wispy and thin, like the peanut man's whistle or a lone frog cheeping in the twilight. And now it roared out, sounding like the shouts of boys yelling under a raft in the water.

And in Wallie Bangs' house his wireless seemed to answer Joey's in a frenzied kind of way.

"Dot-da-dot-dot!" said Joey's.

"Da-dot! Da-dot!" answered Wallie Bangs'.

They are having a conversation, thought Jane, in a funny kind of a language. Maybe she would get as fond of radio as her brothers. She could save up her money or the soap coupons perhaps, and get another pair of ear phones.

She listened again to the children in the yard in back. There were fewer voices now. Some of the children must have gone home.

"Come home! Come home! Wherever you are!" It was Nancy. It sounded as though she were breaking up the game. Probably Mrs. Stokes had called her and Beatrice in. Jane waited a little longer. Nancy might still come to the back fence and whistle, a long high note and a shorter low one. And they would be best friends again beginning tonight, daylight saving time eve. But nobody whistled, and feeling very disconsolate Jane went into the house and up the stairs to her brothers' bedroom.

She sat down on their white iron bed. She watched Joey and Rufus, heads bent over their wireless, gently sliding the contact back and forth, back and forth. They didn't seem to hear or notice her come in at all, they were so absorbed.

"D'ya hear that?" came Wallie Bangs' laconic voice.

"Yeh . . . comin' in good . . . " said Joe.

All of a sudden Joey and Rufus slid their contact back and forth excitedly. They must be going to "get" something, thought Jane. The code signals were making a desperate chatter.

They made Jane laugh, they sounded so funny. "Sh-sh!" said Joey, frowning at her. "It's nearly time for the Arlington time signal."

"I wish I could hear it," said Jane. "I never have heard it."

Joey put his finger to his lips and frowned at her. Then he beckoned her to him. Then he held his hand up. Stop! Like a traffic policeman. Then he beckoned her to him again.

Jane approached cautiously. Joey pulled his ear phones half off, put them back on, then off completely and stuck them hastily on Jane's braids.

"D'ya hear it?" he asked enthusiastically. "Arlin'ton time signal!"

Jane heard an excited bz-z-z-zz-z burst upon her ears. And the Arlington time signal was over. Joey's and Rufus' eyes were shining.

"Gee . . . thanks," said Jane. She took the ear phones off and sat down on the bed again.

So that was the Arlington time signal! Well . . . Did she like the Arlington time signal well enough to spend all her time tuning in? Well . . . She wished they'd find music on the radio.

But Joey and Rufus were wrapped up in it

again. They had forgotten about her being there. Rufus' head was nodding. These late hours he was keeping with Joey to hear the Arlington time signal were telling on him.

Jane looked around the boys' room. On a shelf was a megaphone. Some Yale man, happy over beating Harvard, had given it to Joey after the football game. An idea danced through Jane's head. She would like to take the megaphone, get under the bed, and imitate the Arlington time signal; do it again for the boys since they loved it so.

But goodness! What was she thinking? Radio was a serious business . . . no April Fool's stunts about it. Silence fell upon the room except for the static. Now it was wispy and wan . . . a sleepy sound . . . Now it whistled. A long high note and a shorter low note. Best friends. That's what it sounded like. Like Nancy's whistle. Jane felt sad again. Radio was all right. Fine in fact. A serious business though, Joey had said once. She wasn't being serious if she thought about April Fool's stunts with a megaphone. There was that whistle again. Funny how much like Nancy's whistle the static was sounding. A long high note and a shorter low one . . . real loud now. Jane listened sharply. Could it be . . . Why! It was real! It was Nancy Stokes! Best friends! It wasn't static! Or was she dreaming?

She ran down the stairs and out the back door, slamming it. She stood on the back stoop listening.

She heard nothing. She must have imagined it. Or was it the static after all? Of course Nancy must be in bed by now. Janey had heard the last, "Come home! Come home! Wherever you are," a long time ago.

She turned to go in. As she did so, yes! It was unmistakable. Nancy's whistle. A long high note and a shorter low one. Jane answered it. Nancy couldn't be going to say, "Jane is a pain," because there wasn't anybody around to say it in front of. Jane ran to the back fence and climbed up.

"Hey, Janey!" said Nancy. "Where are you?"

"Here, on the fence."

"Oh . . . Well, I just wanted to tell you you were right. You were right to stick up for Beatrice because she really was right. I sure was mad, but you were right."

"I suppose I should have stuck up for you," said Jane apologetically.

"No. You were right. You stuck up for Beatrice even though you're my best friend. That's bravery."

Jane squirmed her toes around in her shoes and said nothing.

"Here," said Nancy abruptly. "Here's my ring. It's red, sort of like a ruby. It's a friendship ring. That shows we're best friends."

Jane took the ring and put it on her finger. Best friends again!

"Well, so long," said Nancy.

"So long," said Jane, turning the ring around on her finger.

"How about looking for wild flowers on Shingle Hill tomorrow? We have an extra hour with

this daylight saving time. We might find the first hepatica."

"Yeh, Shingle Hill . . ." said Jane.

"Well, so long!"

"So long."

11

THE BIG CELEBRATION

Flags were flying everywhere! Balloon men, popcorn men, and peanut sellers went up and down the streets! An organ-grinder with his monkey was in town! The children were let out of school! The bank was closed! A holiday for all! And why? Because today was the oldest inhabitant's hundredth birthday. One hundred years old! A century!

Jane sat on the curb in front of the library. She had been sitting here for hours, waiting for the parade. In one hand she was holding a flag. In the other she was holding the oldest inhabitant's birthday present. Jane hoped he would like this present. As a matter of fact you could really call it a hundred presents she had for him.

When Jane was ten years old, she had gotten ten presents. Of course, she had counted the box of handkerchiefs that Sylvie gave her as six presents, because there were six in the box. Rufus had said this was wrong. She should have counted them as only one present unless the six handkerchiefs came in six different boxes. Nevertheless, counting them as six made ten presents she had received. The oldest inhabitant was ten times ten. He should have one hundred presents.

Well, he would. That is, if you could count a clump of one hundred bluets as one hundred presents. She didn't ask Rufus, but Jane thought you could. When she saw this clump of bluets in the field in back of the library yesterday, she wondered if by any chance it had a hundred flowers to it. And it had! One hundred exactly. Jane was amazed. She had counted them twice to make sure. So she carefully dug it up and made a basket for it out of purple thistles.

Jane started to count the bluets, hoping none had fallen off during the night. Thirty-nine, forty . . . oh, they must all still be here. She leaned forward to see if the parade was coming yet. She strained her ears, thinking she heard the band. No. Not coming yet.

It had been hard not to give the oldest inhabitant his present yesterday. Janey had run back and forth from her house to his several times. Once she had not been able to resist telling him she had a present for him.

"In fact, you might call it one hundred presents," she had added. Then she was sorry she had told him. He might get so impatient and not be able to sleep. That's what happened to her before birthdays and Christmas. Well, now he had waited and so had she, and she could give him his present as soon as she had the chance. She hoped that she could give it to him at eleven-forty-five on the dot. That is when he would be one hundred exactly.

More people were arriving. They lined the streets. Jane was glad she was sitting on the curb, right in the front. She took off her sandal to empty out the gravel. As she was buckling it up again, her eyes fell on a penny in the gutter.

A penny, half hidden in the dirt. Jane picked it up and rubbed it off. She looked to see if there were any more. She wished she'd look down and see a row of pennies stretching straight ahead, one touching the next. And the line of pennies would not end. It would reach down Rock Avenue and around the corner as far as . . . oh . . . it would never end. Ouch! Jane's back ached with the thought of picking up these pennies. Sometimes she found one penny, but the line always ended there just as this one had. At one.

Jane polished the penny on her sock. It was

too bad she couldn't find a hundred pennies. On every one of her birthdays she received as many pennies as she was years old. She liked to shake  them in her hand and try to make them sound the way coins did in Mama's palm. It would be nice to be able to give the oldest inhabitant one hundred pennies since he was one hundred years old. Well, she had the hundred bluets. If only he wouldn't be like Rufus and think unless they came in one hundred baskets they should count as only one present. Jane stuck the penny in the basket. That would surprise him, that penny!

She stood up and stretched her back. And she looked hard way down the street. The parade? No, it wasn't coming around the corner yet. 'Way at the very end of the street the blue water of the Sound sparkled in the sunshine.

Jane's heart beat fast. Just the idea of the parade excited her, and it hadn't even begun yet. At first when Jane heard there was going to be a big celebration for the oldest inhabitant, she thought of course it would be held in the Yale Bowl. Once she had been in a pageant in the Yale Bowl. She had been one of the waves. Thousands of little girls dressed in blue and green cheese cloth had swayed back and forth, back and forth, so the people in the audience would think they were waves in the ocean. Close up the girls did not look like waves. Jane knew all the girls around her. They were all in Room Four. And they did not look like waves. Fortunately from a distance they did. Jane was sorry the celebration was not going to be in the Yale Bowl. She would like to have been a wave for the oldest inhabitant.

Even so, this was very exciting. More and more people were crowding the walks. They all craned their necks. Was that the parade coming now? No, it was the milk-man's horse and wagon.

Jane was not going to march in this parade. She was just going to watch it. She could have marched with her school class or the girls of the junior basketball team. Nancy Stokes was riding in an automobile in the parade because her father was one of the town selectmen, a dignitary. Not Jane. She would not ride or march. She would keep herself free in order to be of any possible service to the oldest inhabitant. He had reached the age of one hundred. True! Even so, she was going to be on the alert and help him if necessary. . . .

Boom! Boom! Bd-loom, boom, boom!

The parade! Here it was, coming around the corner! Prickly feelings ran up and down Jane's spine. Tears popped into her eyes. She danced up and down.

Boom! Boom!

Oh, she hoped the band would play. A policeman on a dappled-gray horse kept the crowd in place on the curb.

First came the town militia carrying the colors. And the band struck up just as it reached the library. The blast from the big brass horns vibrated in Janey's ears. Her legs kept going up and down, up and down, and there wasn't any teacher clapping and making them march either. They just couldn't help it.

Next came the Moose men from Moose Hall with their band. Then the Indians from Wampum Lodge, dancing and waving tomahawks. Jane drew back into the crowd. Were they real?

Next the Masons and the Elks, with bands of their own.

Then Chief Mulligan of the police force, swinging his stick.

Then a lot of other policemen. Where did they come from, Jane wondered. Maybe from New Haven . . . and policemen on horses!

Next came the town selectmen in their automobiles. Jane waved her flag at Nancy. She knew a lot of people in this parade. Nancy, her best friend, and the oldest inhabitant . . . Was he coming now in one of these big automobiles? No, not yet.

Then came the firemen's band and the fire-engines. Not only the Cranbury engines, but shining ones from all the neighboring towns; some that were drawn by horses still, and some of the new automobile fire-engines. Also the first steam boiler of the Town of Cranbury. And running along the side, Bosie, the fire department's dog.

Then came the veterans of the Civil War. The oldest inhabitant called these veterans "children," for none of them had even reached the age of ninety yet. But the oldest inhabitant wasn't riding with them. He wasn't coming yet, though people were craning their necks looking for him.

Jane liked it best when the bands played. Sometimes you could still hear one band up ahead playing one thing and another band would march into sight playng something else.

Now came the Governor's foot-guard and the foot-guard's band. And the band struck up "The Stars and Stripes Forever!"

Now a murmur was running up the street through the crowds. "Here he comes! Here he comes!" they yelled, craning their necks.

And then the oldest inhabitant really did come,

in a shiny black car, nodding slowly to left and to right.

Jane waved lustily. And she cried "Hurrah for Hannibal B. Buckle!" along with everybody else. She held her present high for him to see, too. So he would know she was not fooling yesterday when she told him she had one for him.

The oldest inhabitant saw her. And he played Hawkshaw, the detective. Imagine! On his one hundredth birthday! And then his limousine rolled on. The shouts of "Hurrah for Hannibal B. Buckle!" were caught up farther along the street, and farther still until they grew fainter and fainter, and now the next band drowned them out.

Jane decided to stay here and watch the rest

of the parade go by. Then she would take a short-cut, catch up with the oldest inhabitant's part of the parade, and give him his present at eleven-forty-five on the dot.

Now came the Boy Scouts with their band; the Girl Scouts with theirs; the Campfire Girls; the Naval Reserve boys in the white middy blouses Mama had made for them; the fife and drum corps.

Next came the ladies of the Red Cross, the ladies of the Eastern Star, the ladies of P'fessor Fairweather's Browning Society. Jane saw Mrs. Price and waved to her.

Floats were going by now, floats that showed different scenes in the life of the oldest inhabitant.

Then came a great many little girls all dressed in white, and all carrying flowers, and next a great many little boys carrying flags. Last of all came many children who weren't really in the parade but who couldn't help marching. Clara Pringle was dragging Brud in his red express wagon, and Brud was holding a red balloon.

That was the end of the parade, for here came the street cleaners in their white canvas uniforms.

Jane tore through the town and caught up with the parade at Main Street. Since she was not part of this parade, Janey thought she should

just walk the way she did in real life, not march. However, she could not help her legs moving up and down in time to the band, and she soon fell into step, marching as close to the oldest inhabitant's automobile as the policeman on the horse would let her.

And now the parade was nearing the Green. Jane looked around. What a crowd! You would hardly recognize the Green. Daisy garlands and flags everywhere. And there was a large sign at the entrance:

CRANBURY IS PROUD OF
HANNIBAL B. BUCKLE

The oldest inhabitant was mounting the grand-

stand now. Jane looked up at him. Suddenly the
church bells rang out, peal after peal. Jane looked
at the clock on the church. Eleven-forty-five! He
had reached the age of one hundred! A century!
Jane looked at him and she looked at her basket.
Now was the time to give it to him. But how?
All the town dignitaries and the superintendent
of schools were surrounding him and shaking
hands.

Jane sighed. She would like to give him his
present now. She had been holding it so tightly
it was really beginning to wilt. Two thistles had
gotten lost out of the handle. Jane hoped she
had not lost any of the bluets. She went over to
the drinking trough thinking a little water would
freshen the present. But she quickly darted back
to the front line for the speeches had begun.

The speeches were very short, even Mr. Pennypepper's. Jane was almost sorry when he stopped
for he was such a jolly sight when he gave a
speech. He rocked from heel to toe, rattled the
keys and the coins in his pocket, and fixed his
eyes now on the tip-top of the steeple of the
church and now on the flag waving on the top of
the flagpole.

After he spoke, a very little girl in Room One
presented the oldest inhabitant with a huge sil-

ver cup, a gift from all the school children. Jane herself had given a penny towards it. So had Sylvie and Joey and Rufus. Four pennies in all from the four Moffats. Even so Jane was glad she also had this basket for him. If she could only give it to him.

It was too bad Mr. Pennypepper did not know about the bluets. If he did he might call on her. He had a list in his hands. Now this one, now that one, he called . . . but she was not on the list.

Jane ran over to the drinking trough again to revive the wilting bluets. They were still pretty, she decided.

But goodness! A tremendous cheer burst upon the air. The oldest inhabitant himself! He was speaking now. What would he think if she were not there to hear him recite his piece? Jane ducked back and regained her position. Again she held the basket forward. Perhaps he would see it and know it was his.

The oldest inhabitant's voice was very faint and nobody could hear what he said. Jane watched his mouth go up and down and knew he was talking. Nobody really cared whether they heard him or not though. They only wanted to see him. Jane listened hard all the same. She thought she heard him say her name. She thought she heard him say at the end, "and especially I want to thank Jane, the mysterious middle Moffat, for all she has . . ." Then Janey could not hear any more. She was embarrassed. He was thanking her and she hadn't even given him anything yet. She looked around to see if anybody else had heard what he said. Apparently not, or they would all be staring at her in surprise.

The oldest inhabitant sat down. And the loudest cheers and applause so far rang out. The band began to play, the church bells pealed, and gradually the crowd broke up.

Now everybody was going to get a piece of cake. It was on a table in front of the white church. The oldest inhabitant was to cut the first slice, of course. Jane thought that then she would surely have a chance to give him his present. So she ducked in and out of the crowd and she finally arrived at the cake. What a birthday cake! Seven stories to it, a hundred blue candles burning on it, and his name, Hannibal B. Buckle, in gold letters.

Hannibal B. Buckle! The oldest inhabitant! But where was he? Jane looked around for him anxiously. Her hand was feeling shriveled and cramped. She would like to change her basket

for a piece of this wonderful cake. Thank goodness, she thought, this was not a wedding; not a wedding, but a hundredth birthday party and everybody could eat his cake. They didn't have to sleep on it.

Where was the oldest inhabitant? Jane began to feel guilty. What kind of taking care of the oldest inhabitant was this? While she was ducking around in her efforts to get near this cake, he had become lost in the crowd.

Jane asked herself sternly whether she had really woven her way over here in order to give the oldest inhabitant his birthday present. Or had she had her mind on this wonderful cake?

But at last, accompanied by Mr. Pennypepper and the town selectmen, the oldest inhabitant reached the table. And he cut the first slice of cake! Jane stood right beside him. Now she really did have a chance to give him his present. But suddenly she felt too shy. True, he had played Hawkshaw all year and called her the mysterious middle Moffat. But now he had reached the age of one hundred and all this celebration was for him. Jane held the moist basket in the palm of her hand and wondered what to do with it. She couldn't eat a piece of cake and hold onto it and her flag too.

"Why . . ." said the oldest inhabitant, "here is the mysterious middle Moffat. And is that my present?" Jane handed him the basket. At last! It was as easy as that. And he handed her a piece of cake.

"My," said the oldest inhabitant, "this is a nice present. A hundred presents really! Now come along. Party's over. You live on my street. We'll ride home together."

A ride in an automobile! Jane had had a ride in an automobile only three times before in her life. Where were the other Moffats? There was such a crowd she could not see them. She wished they could come too. Rufus had never had a ride in an automobile.

Jane smoothed her hair and her dress. She was going to ride with Cranbury's most honored citizen. She sucked in her breath. A dignitary! That's just what she would be.

Jane and the oldest inhabitant stepped into the limousine. They waited for Miss Buckle and the driver to come. The oldest inhabitant held his basket on his knees and Jane held her flag.

"Now that you have reached the age of one hundred, do you think you will try for two hundred?" Jane asked.

"Yes," he said, "I think so. What do you think?"

"Oh, I would," said Jane. "And they might celebrate that birthday in the Yale Bowl. Maybe then I could be a wave."

The oldest inhabitant nodded. And he nodded practically the whole way home. As they rode along, people waved and cheered. Jane sat scrunched up tight in the back of the seat and looked nei-

ther to the left nor the right. She did not want
people to think she considered any of this cheering was for her.

Oh! There was Mama! Mama and the rest of
the Moffats! They were all looking at her in
astonishment. She gave them a quick apologetic
wave. She hoped they could see that she wished
they were here in this car, having a ride too.
However, to her delight, Mr. Buckle stopped the
driver.

"Get in. Get in!" he said to all the Moffats. "We'll all ride home together."

It was lucky this automobile had extra seats. The driver just pulled them out of the floor in front of the back seat. Mama and Sylvie sat on these two seats. Rufus and Joey climbed into the front seat beside the driver and the driver let Rufus blow the automobile horn at the corners. Jane sat in the middle, between Mr. Buckle and his daughter. She smiled at the oldest inhabitant. He didn't look any different than yesterday when he was only ninety-nine. Jane felt happy. What a nice way for the big celebration to end, everybody riding in an automobile!

And slowly the limousine rolled home.